Mad About Jack

*For Barbara —
Thanks for
everything you
do!*

*Love,
Gayle*

Mad About Jack

Gayle Kasper

Five Star • Waterville, Maine

First Edition
First Printing: September 2005

Published in 2005 in conjunction with Tekno Books.

Set in 11 pt. Plantin by Liana M. Walker.

Printed in the United States on permanent paper.

Library of Congress Cataloging-in-Publication Data

Kasper, Gayle.
    Mad about Jack / by Gayle Kasper.—1st ed.
      p. cm.
    ISBN 1-59414-295-5 (hc : alk. paper)
    1. Competition (Psychology)—Fiction. 2. Automobile dealers—Fiction. 3. Used car trade—Fiction. I. Title.
    PS3611.A7856M33 2005
    813'.6—dc22   2005013400

Dedication

For Mad Jack—and all the women he's charmed,
especially my critique buddies through the years,
Kitty, Karen, Carla, Marilyn, Judy, Sally, Chris,
Sarah, Jo and Marcie.
Also for Bob, my wonderful husband of thirty years—
who puts up with me when my head is in the clouds.

Dedication

Chapter One

Holly Hanford swung her vintage white Thunderbird into her private parking space at the side of the building. She gathered up her purse and her briefcase filled with the sales figures she'd taken home and pored over last evening. As she'd expected, she'd been pleased with the numbers.

Jack Murdock, her irksome competition, had been a prickly thorn in her side ever since he set up shop across the street a few months before—but fortunately his unorthodox sales tactics had done very little damage to her business.

At least, so far.

As she rounded the front of the building she saw her entire sales force gaping through the showroom window as if a natural disaster had struck across the street.

Secretly Holly hoped an earthquake had swallowed up Jack Murdock and his whole commercial venture, but since McCallum, Texas did not sit on a major fault line, she supposed there was very little likelihood of that.

Her curious gaze followed that of her staff's. Jack Murdock, wearing a sports jacket wild enough to halt the four lanes of traffic racing along Woodland Avenue, was directing the installation of a new sign over his sales office.

In spite of his doubtful taste in clothing, he managed to

look totally male, Holly noted. It was amazing what a broad pair of shoulders could do for orange plaid.

Quickly she checked the direction of her thoughts and wrenched her gaze away from the man's lean, solid frame, zeroing in on the sign instead.

How had she missed noticing it first anyway?

The display blazoned the wordage MAD JACK'S USED AUTOS in giant letters and featured a crazy caricature of Jack himself, all done in brilliant neon. A series of multicolored flashing lights chased each other around the perimeter of the sign.

T. R. Kimball, her top salesman, joined her outside, carrying a spare cup of hot coffee. "I thought you might need this," he said, offering her the Styrofoam container.

Holly looked up into the older man's sympathetic face. "Only if it's laced with something stronger than caffeine," she replied, but accepted it readily.

T.R. ran his fingers through his thinning red hair and nodded at the gaudy display across the street. "That thing's big enough to cause a power outage over a ten-block area," he said.

"It's not funny, T.R. That thing's a blatant monstrosity."

She glanced up at the newly updated blue-and-white sign she'd hung over her own place a few weeks earlier. HANFORD MOTORS in unpretentious block letters gleamed back at her.

"That man tries to outdo me at every turn," she said, giving in to the hot wave of indignation welling up inside her. "I put up a new sign, he puts up one three times the size. I offer two free tickets to the dinner playhouse for a trade-in, he offers four."

"It's a little game called one-upmanship," T.R. explained with a rueful smile.

"For which he writes all the rules. Well, I don't intend to play his little game."

With one final scowl at the blinking wonder across the street, she stormed inside the showroom and into her private office, slamming the door behind her.

She needed to put Jack Murdock, and his crazy enterprise, out of her mind. She had a business to run—and she didn't have time for one nuisance hunk of a man, with an overdose of male charm and good looks, to distract her.

The used car trade in this town was competitive, yet none of the other dealers she knew played quite as ruthlessly as this man.

Was he trying to drive her out of business?

"Fat chance!" she said aloud.

She'd worked too hard these past two years, turning Hanford Motors into the success that it was, to allow Jack Murdock to come along now and ruin things for her.

Jack Murdock pushed his way through the front door of Hanford Motors, treating Holly's sales crew to a breezy wave. "Just came by to see your Boss Lady," he said. "Is she in her office?"

He was feeling expansive about his big, new sign and in the mood to gloat—just a little.

"She is. But I doubt she'll be thrilled to see *you*, Murdock," T.R. said before turning his attention back to the stack of paperwork on his desk.

Jack gave a low throaty chuckle. He'd like to have T. R. Kimball working for him. The man could sell cars; but he was loyal to Holly—and not overly fond of Jack. Neither Holly, nor T.R., was pleased with him—not since he'd stolen Holly's best mechanic away last week. But business was business, after all.

As if he were a man scouting out enemy territory, Jack's canny gaze swept around the showroom. Holly kept a couple of older classics on the sales floor, all with hefty sticker prices, as if she didn't really want to sell them. He suspected she didn't.

It was a damned attractive sales office, all done in blues and cream. Pictures of vintage autos lined the walls. Overhead three large chandeliers offered soft lighting instead of the usual fluorescent glare. The lady had style he had to admit. Beauty and savvy, Holly Hanford had both.

He rapped once on her half-closed office door, then pushed it open.

Holly was seated at her desk, lost in thought, her dark head bent over an inventory printout. Her hair was the rich warm color of maple syrup. Jack appraised the way she wound one sensuous curl around her finger as she worked. He wondered at its softness, his fingers itching to confirm its texture.

A faint whiff of her scent filled the room. Jack couldn't place the fragrance—but it had the same subtle elegance as the woman who wore it.

"I came over to see if you noticed my new sign," he said, easing his tall frame through the door.

She looked up at the sound of his voice and her jewel green eyes flashed, then darkened warily. Yes, the anger was there. He saw it in the set of her luscious lips, the way her chest rose, her firm round breasts pushing against the magenta silk of her blouse.

A smaller version of the chandeliers in the showroom hung over her mahogany desk, its light casting creamy shadows over the heated flush of her skin. If it wasn't for that un-neighborly expression on her pretty face, he could spend the rest of his day just standing here looking at her.

10

She stood up haughtily behind her desk. Her slim, off-white skirt clung to her hips tantalizingly enough to torment any man between the ages of eighteen and eighty. At thirty-two Jack was definitely affected.

"If you're referring to that flashing . . . *billboard* of yours, how could I have missed it?" Her voice had an edge, he noticed, but then it usually lost its dulcet tone whenever she addressed him.

"Billboard?" He splayed a hand over his chest as if she'd mortally wounded him. "I thought it brought a little color to the neighborhood."

"Color?" Holly sat back down in stunned disbelief as visions of that vibrant-hued sign of his swam riotously before her eyes.

"Yeah—it'll bring in the customers. They'll be able to spot the thing from miles away," he defended, leaning forward over her desk, his hands resting firmly on its polished surface.

A rakish smile slid across his face. Straight white teeth and a deep dimple in his right cheek only increased the charisma. Holly could see why people—women, at least—bought cars from this man.

His hands were broad and strong as they rested on the desk, and for a moment she found herself wondering how they would feel on her—touching her, caressing—

She jerked back her thoughts, angry that she found him so brashly appealing. She tried to ignore the electric blue of his eyes, as well as his fractured reasoning. "Is that your motive, Jack? Or are you just determined to outdo me once again?"

The smile and the dimple deepened. "What's the matter, Hanford? Afraid of a little competition?"

At the moment it wasn't competition but Jack, and the effect he had on her, that frightened her—but she couldn't let

11

him know that. Never again would she let a man see she was vulnerable.

She raised her eyes to his defiantly. "Not honest, forthright competition. But going behind my back to entice Luther Anderson away from me to run your repair department is dirty dealing, however."

"Hey, the guy has mouths to feed."

Her eyes narrowed at him. "You offered him more money?" She knew Luther had a wife and three kids. If Jack could afford to pay him more than Holly, she could hardly blame Luther for leaving. In fact, she'd applaud Jack's offer—no matter how much she hated losing a valued mechanic.

"Well, no. Not exactly. Not to start anyway—"

"Just a promise of more, a promise you won't deliver."

"I always deliver on a promise, Holly. If you'd give yourself a chance to get to know me, you'd find that out."

She frowned, certain she didn't want to get to know Jack better than she already did. "Jack Murdock, if one of the cars on your lot had a flat tire you'd point out that it was only flat on the bottom. Don't try to pull the wool over my eyes. I'm not one of your gullible customers."

He chuckled, a low sexy rumble that vibrated through her like thunder, all the way to her toes. She hated to admit it, but she liked the sound of his laugh.

Just then there was a sharp rap on her office door and T.R. poked his head inside. "Holly, I'm sorry to intrude." He shot Jack a belligerent glower as if to remind the man he'd overstayed his welcome. "But I need your approval on these credit applications."

"Thanks, T.R. I'll look them over." Holly didn't know why she felt so distracted, but suddenly she did—as if T.R. had interrupted something between her and Jack. But there was nothing to interrupt—just a conversation between two adversaries. "Jack was just leaving, weren't you, Jack?"

His gaze locked with hers for an endless moment, then a grin lifted the corners of his wide, sexy mouth. "That's right," he answered. "Gotta go. The new sign's probably dragged in half the town by now, every one of 'em waiting to snap up one of my hot buys."

Hot buys? Holly silenced the groan that threatened to escape her throat. She doubted that the paying public was lined up across the street, but if the likelihood of it would get Jack out of her office, she'd leave his delusion intact.

"I'm sure they are, Jack," she said in her sweetest tone, then watched with an all-too-eager fascination as he strode out the door with a roving, easy swagger. The man was well-muscled masculinity—six perfectly proportioned feet of it, she'd guess, judging by the way he cleared the doorframe.

It was several minutes before her mind focused on the papers T.R. waggled in front of her and several more before she could speak. "That man is trouble, T.R.," she said, taking the credit apps from him.

She needed to stay focused. She had a business to run, and it didn't pay to get distracted, not by one ruggedly handsome male with a dangerous brand of charm.

"You haven't forgotten the retirement party for Brewer Phillips tonight, have you?" T.R. asked before turning to leave.

It was a party Holly didn't want to miss. Brewer owned a competing sales lot—but he'd been a good friend to her father and a good friend to Holly, helping her get Hanford Motors back on its feet after her father's death two years before. She owed him a lot.

"No, I haven't forgotten, T.R. I wouldn't miss Brewer's farewell bash for anything."

13

"Good—why don't I swing by and pick you up after I close up here?"

T.R. was just old-fashioned enough to think a twenty-seven-year-old woman shouldn't go about in the evening un-escorted, and Holly was just feminine enough to enjoy his quaint gallantry.

"I'd like that," she told him.

Alone in her office at last, Holly felt a sudden restlessness. Her thoughts returned to Jack Murdock—a man definitely lacking in quaint gallantry, she was sure.

She paused at the window that fronted Woodland Avenue and peered across the street at Mad Jack's lot. The monster sign blinked off and on—a blinding beacon she'd like to short-circuit.

Was he trying to put her out of business? Or did he just enjoy besting a woman? Whichever it was, Holly wasn't about to let him have the upper hand.

The evening air was already warm for May. Spring was fading rapidly. Sizzling summer days and hot sultry nights were just around the corner, but tonight the weather was perfect. The party for Brewer Phillips had spilled over to the hotel's outdoor pool, the guests enjoying the last vestiges of spring's weather.

Jack sipped his bourbon and soaked up the warm night air, all the while keeping an eye out for newly arriving guests. He'd come tonight to offer his best wishes to Brewer, and that being done, he could have left, but he'd thought Holly would be here. In fact, he'd have bet the keys to his lowest-mileage convertible on it.

She and Brewer were close, he knew. Brewer offered her advice, but from what Jack had seen of her operation, Holly didn't need any. Was it her provocative femininity that drew

14

in the customers? Whatever it was, she didn't need any flashy signs to sell cars. Just her wide sensual smile would do it.

He lifted his drink, ice cubes clinking, and took a slow swallow, enjoying the way the good bourbon slid down his throat. Then over the rim of his glass he saw motion, grace and beauty floating regally through the patio doors toward the pool area.

Holly.

She was a vision in an emerald silk pantsuit that matched the color of her eyes, her long brown hair falling softly to her shoulders, a swirl of rich color with each movement of her head.

She smiled at everyone, and they all responded, eager to speak to her. Freshness and light, Holly reminded him of a cool summer morning.

Holly was instantly aware of Jack standing by the pool, a drink in hand. He'd shed that ugly orange-plaid jacket of his. She saw it gracing the back of a pool chair and thought how much better it looked there.

Without it, however, the man was all the more devastating, his black hair a dramatic foil for that snowy white shirt that hugged his torso, hinting at hard male muscles beneath.

Holly didn't think she'd ever seen a man more infuriatingly good-looking. Or who stole her attention the way this man could. What was it about him? His male good looks? His irreverent, half-skewed view of life? That laidback attitude about anything the least bit serious?

She caught the sound of her name and realized T.R. was speaking to her. "I'm sorry," she said, wrenching her gaze away from Jack and her thoughts back to the conversation T.R. had been one-sidedly conducting. "Did you say something?"

Her evening's escort regarded her with a curious lift of one eyebrow. "I was saying it looks like there's quite a turnout for Brewer tonight," he repeated.

"Yes," she answered. One more than she'd hoped, she thought, her gaze returning to Jack.

What was he doing here? He hadn't mentioned this morning that he planned to attend. Knowing Jack he'd probably shamelessly wangled an invitation so he could check out his competition.

Namely *her*.

She only hoped that he stayed on that side of the pool and she would stay on this side. Then she might be able to survive the evening. But before that thought could become firmly planted in her mind, she saw him approaching. She was reminded of a lone hunter, moving single-mindedly toward its prey—his stride long and easy as he headed straight for T.R. and her.

Holly swallowed hard.

Escape was out of the question.

"I was hoping you'd be here tonight," he said, addressing her directly, as though T.R. were not at her side.

"I was hoping you *wouldn't* be."

Her reply seemed to set him back on his heels for a moment. She enjoyed his temporary loss of aplomb. T.R. seemed to enjoy it, too. She hadn't missed the strangled laugh that came off as a polite cough he hid behind his hand.

"Aw, now, Hanford—is that any way to talk to your competition?" he said, lifting her chin with one finger.

It was Holly's turn to feel a loss of composure. His light touch shot through her like lightning during a hot summer storm, galvanizing her to the spot. She sensed, rather than saw, the frown on T.R.'s face—and hoped neither he, nor Jack, was aware of her quick reaction.

16

All air had fled from her lungs and her heart picked up its pace. She needed to stay calm. This was Jack, a man who could rub her the wrong way with very little trying.

"Jack Murdock, you and your derelict used cars are hardly competition for me," she answered him tartly.

"Maybe. Maybe not. Can I get you a drink?" he asked. This time he included T.R. in the conversation, offering him that charming smile Holly was beginning to hate.

"Not for me," T.R. replied gruffly. She had the feeling her evening escort would love to deck Jack where he stood.

"Hanford?" Jack waited for her answer, smiling at her with those fathomless blue eyes and his overabundant charm.

"A glass of white wine," she said, surprising herself with her reply. She didn't want to drink with this man. He was trouble. And trouble was something she didn't need.

But then, maybe the wine would dull the few sensory brain cells that seemed to pique her attraction to Jack.

Jack guided her to the bar before she could change her mind. He was glad to leave the annoying T.R. behind. Now he could fully appreciate Holly's subtle scent, the feel of her smooth, soft skin as he planted his hand at the small of her back. Even from this distance he could feel T.R.'s disapproving scowl.

He couldn't blame the man. A woman like Holly needed protection—especially from a man like Jack. He dragged his gaze away from the clingy silk that shimmered like green fire over the tempting outline of her breasts, and smiled up at the burly bartender instead. The scenery wasn't nearly as pretty, but it was definitely safer.

"White wine for the countess," he said. "And another bourbon for me."

"A *half* glass of wine," Holly said from behind him and the

17

bartender obliged her with a nod and a smile.

A few moments later Jack handed Holly her drink and deftly guided her away from the crowd at the bar. "It's cooler out by the pool," he said, edging her in that direction.

"Yes," she agreed.

The emerald silk whispered around her long legs and Jack hoped the night breeze would air-condition his libido. Holly had it heated up and running full blast like no woman had in a while—a long while.

"Countess?" she asked when they were once again out under the stars.

The moonlight glistened in her hair and turned her skin creamier than a rich strand of pearls—the real thing, not the white fake ones he offered a woman to test drive one of his autos. "It's how I think of you. Cool and regal, someone to admire from afar—like a countess."

Holly was taken aback. Cool and regal was not how she thought of herself. Vulnerable, a little unsure of herself, but determined, gutsy perhaps—that would better sum up Holly Hanford. Plus smart—smart enough to recognize one of Jack's lines.

And not a very good one at that.

She took a sip of her wine, observing him over the top of her glass. If she knew more about her competitor she might be better prepared for his next move, an edge she could use. "Tell me, Jack, with all the locations around this town, why did you choose to open up shop across the street from my place?"

"Where better, Countess?" He gave her a wide smile.

Any place would be better and Holly would like to suggest a few. "Well, you managed to single-handedly create a market glut. Our little stretch of Woodland Avenue can't handle two competing sales lots."

"Oh, but it can very easily. It's a kind of one-stop shopping. When customers don't get what they want from your side of the street, they come over to mine."

"I see. And why wouldn't they get what they want from me?"

"Because, Hanford, whatever offer you make, I improve on and then, bingo, I sell cars."

The man made some kind of frightening sense, but she didn't dare let him see that it bothered her. She raised her chin coolly. "Then I'll just have to make certain my customers find no need to shop elsewhere. If you'll excuse me, I see Brewer over there and I haven't yet offered my congratulations."

There it was—that countess look, he thought. Cool and regal. Could he break through to the woman beneath? And if he did, what would he find there?

Damned if he didn't want to know.

"See you later, Countess," he said, lifting his glass in a sort of salute.

Holly walked away uneasily. She wasn't sure if the man was a threat or a nuisance. Until tonight she'd considered him nothing more than a nuisance, but now she wasn't so sure.

She thought about his intense blue eyes and dazzle-a-woman smile. Too bad he didn't look more like the crazy caricature of himself atop his gargantuan sign—then she might be better able to deal with him.

"Holly."

Brewer Phillips wrapped her in a bear hug and she suddenly felt safe from unsettling men like Jack Murdock. When she'd freed herself from Brewer's warm embrace she looked up into his craggy face and smiled. "Are you sure you don't want to reconsider this retirement idea of yours? It won't be the same without you in the fray."

Until that moment she hadn't realized just how much she'd miss him—and his sage advice.

"I won't be too far away, Holly. If you need me just check the nearest creek bank. I'll be sitting there with my rod and reel."

Holly hoped she wouldn't need to ask for his help, but considering that her wily opponent could very well give Hanford Motors serious trouble, she might need some advice. "I hope you enjoy fishing, Brewer. You've earned your retirement."

She said a brief hello to Brad, Brewer's son, who'd taken over for his father. The change gave Holly some misgivings. Brad was not half the man his father was, and she doubted he ever would be. She only hoped Brewer knew what he was doing, placing his son in charge. But maybe that was unfair— she didn't really know that much about Brad Phillips.

Besides, could he be any worse than the blight to the neighborhood—Jack Murdock?

She scanned the crowd for a quick glimpse of her annoying rival and found him talking to a group of people who sold television-advertising time. Brewer had done some commercials in the past—and she supposed Jack was considering the same course of action. No doubt he'd choose to star in the thirty-second spots himself—with every female within viewing range tuning in.

And if they all trooped to his lot to buy cars from Mad Jack?

Holly could soon be out of business.

She put that unsettling thought out of her mind and returned her attention to the rollicking story one of the guests was relating about Brewer in his younger days. Holly laughed with the others, but soon her gaze drifted back across the pool area to Jack.

He stood half a head taller than the other men here tonight and was by far the most handsome, she was forced to admit. With his broad-shouldered frame and coal-dark hair, he made all the others appear nondescript by comparison.

She was just admiring the masculine shape of his ear and the way his hair curled over his white shirt collar when he turned, and their gazes collided. Before she could glance away she caught the quirk of one dark eyebrow and the amused glint in his eyes that asked if she liked what she saw.

Holly fought down the quick rise of color that attacked her cheeks, but to no avail. The unwanted heat took hold. Where was T.R.? It was time to leave.

Past time.

Saying a quick goodbye to the group and to Brewer with a promise to see him again soon, she left the pool area and stepped inside to look for T.R.

The room was deserted except for the bartender who was taking advantage of the slack period to inventory his liquor and glassware. He didn't even look up when Holly deposited her goblet on the tray provided for empties. She hadn't finished all her wine, but still felt slightly out of focus from its effects. If only she'd taken the time to eat something before she'd come tonight.

She needed air, but not the noisy poolside. She opened a pair of French doors and found they led out onto a small balcony. The gentle night breeze blew across her face, reviving her. She could hear the sounds from the party, but they were thankfully muted.

Off in the distance the lights of the town twinkled like diamonds on a jeweler's black-velvet pad. The heady scent of flowers from a small garden two stories below wafted upward,

21

and Holly inhaled deeply. She wished she'd discovered this spot earlier.

"I see you found an escape from the noise."

The voice came from the doorway behind her, low and deep and as deliciously velvet as the night.

"Jack."

She turned, wishing the man would disappear into the dark.

"Am I intruding?"

That was putting it mildly. "It's not a private balcony, if that's what you mean."

"Yeah, but you found it first."

He eased in next to her and his male scent surrounded her. The moonlight danced through his hair, turning it blue-black in the dark night. Their hands were inches apart on the cool, black railing. His shirt-sleeves were rolled back. A sprinkling of crisp, dark hairs glistened over the sinewy length of his forearms. She remembered she'd been about to leave. She *should* leave.

"So I did," she answered.

"And you can decide if you want to share it. Of course, if I make you uncomfortable—"

Her head came up, her eyes narrowing at him. "Uncomfortable?" His flagrant ego would like that, she thought. He'd enjoyed her covert appraisal of him out by the pool earlier.

"Yes, I seem to ruffle your feathers for some unknown reason."

Unknown reason? "Allow me to supply the reason, Mr. Insufferable." She stabbed a finger at his broad chest, then wished she hadn't. It was muscle-hard beneath his shirt, and for a mental moment she imagined it bare, tanned down to a flat, lean stomach and furred with the same dark hair that escaped the V of his white shirt.

22

He raised that dark eyebrow she'd seen earlier. "Enlighten me."

She'd like to do more than that—she'd like to toss him over the railing into the flower bed below. "Ever since the day you moved in on my territory with those bargain-basement hunks of tin, you've been trying to undermine my operation."

"Undermine your operation?"

She'd say it in plain English. "Put me out of business."

"Why, Countess, you wound me—I have no intention of putting you out of business. I just want an honest piece of the pie, that's all. There's no reason we can't peacefully co-exist."

His gaze drifted from her eyes to her mouth, blatantly steadying there for an uneasy moment. She didn't want to co-exist, or anything else, with Jack Murdock.

She turned away from him and stared out into the night. "I saw you talking to the TV people earlier," she said as nonchalantly as she could manage. "Are you planning to do a few commercials?"

"Why do you ask that?"

If he had some big TV blitz planned, she wanted to be prepared for it. "I just want to know what underhanded . . . *surprise* you intend to pull on me next."

That made him smile, a slow dangerous smile that warned her she should run for cover. He was standing close, so close anyone seeing them might think he intended to kiss her—but if Jack Murdock tried that he'd find himself flailing over the balcony faster than he knew what hit him.

If he'd read her thoughts they hadn't frightened him. He reached out and touched her cheek, a mere brush, but quick heat raced like liquid fire through her veins. "You intrigue me, Countess," he said, his voice a low rasp in the night air. "Maybe more than you should."

Chapter Two

Saturday was Holly's busiest day. Sales were usually brisk, and she looked forward to the excitement of the sell, the clinching of the deal. Her cars were clean and roadworthy, her prices fair, and the customers knew it.

But after the little bit of sleep she'd gotten last night, she wasn't sure she was functioning at her best today. Thoughts of her annoying competition had kept her tossing and turning until nearly dawn. She didn't need Jack Murdock in her life right now—not when her business was finally doing well and her life was uncomplicated.

What was it about him that put her so on edge? Was it his presence across the street—or the way he had of reminding her she was a woman?

She didn't want to respond to the man—but last night, on that balcony, in the glittering moonlight, with his lips so close, the male scent of him surrounding her, she nearly had.

But not again.

She intended to be on her guard against Jack Murdock—and his fast-talking charm. The man was a threat to Hanford Motors *and* to Holly's peace of mind.

She hadn't forgotten about Adam, another man with a charming smile and glib words. A man she'd thought she loved. A man she'd thought loved her back.

Adam had been there for her after her father's death—and she'd been so grateful for his help that she hadn't noticed how he'd ingratiated himself into her life and her business until he'd nearly sold her down the river.

It had taken nearly a year for her to recover from the damage that Adam had done to her, both financially and emotionally. But she'd come out of it a stronger, wiser and more determined woman. Determined to run Hanford's her own way. And to avoid men who didn't have her best interests at heart.

Like Jack Murdock, her disreputable, across-the-street rival.

Adam was ancient history now—except for the bitter lesson she'd learned. And she'd never allow herself to be that vulnerable again.

She returned to the paperwork on her desk, her shoulders squared and her determination firmly in place. She'd just finished the last of it when the phone on her desk buzzed insistently. Holly punched the intercom line and T.R.'s husky voice came over it. "We can use your help out here, Holly. The customers are swarming over the lot like bees."

Holly was glad to abandon the paperwork. Her adrenaline was pumping. "Sounds like it's going to be a great day, T.R. I'll be right out."

She didn't know what she'd do without T.R. He kept the lot humming, his finger on everything and Holly trusted him implicitly. It had been her good fortune when he'd signed on shortly after she'd taken over the business. It had been after she'd dismissed Adam and Holly had needed something going her way about then.

He and his wife had moved here to escape the Nebraska winters. Evelyn, his wife, was one of Holly's dearest friends. She ran a small knitting shop on the town square and taught knitting classes there three evenings a week. On the other evenings Holly made sure T.R. didn't pull the after-hours shift, usually taking them herself, so he could be home and the couple could enjoy some time together.

T.R., like her, loved a busy Saturday on the lot. Holly only hoped they stayed busy and her across-the-street rival, Jack Murdock, didn't ruin Hanford's track record.

The morning sunshine greeted her as she stepped through the showroom door. The day was heating up, promising warmer weather and reminding her summer was on its way.

She cast a cursory glance across the street. Only to keep a wary eye on the competition, she told herself. It was motivated by self-preservation, not a desire to catch a glimpse of Jack's lean, hard body.

He was out on the lot showing an SUV to a customer—or knowing Jack, giving the hard sell. He was dressed in another wild sports jacket—this one the color of a ripe eggplant.

Holly stifled a groan.

Over his handsome and well-shaped head, strings of brightly colored banners flapped in the stiff Texas breeze, sounding like a flock of turkeys in take-off. Prospective buyers milled around. One, two, three, she counted. Then she turned to examine her own small place. Seven, she tallied quickly and smiled with satisfaction.

Let the man have his flapping banners and outrageous signs.

Holly started across the lot toward a customer.

Things were going her way.

Three sales later, she glanced up to see Jack striding toward her in that confident, easy swagger of his. He'd shed the appalling jacket and rolled the sleeves of his blue Oxford-cloth shirt up on his tanned forearms.

"Beautiful day today, Hanford," he said, peeling off his trendy sunglasses.

It *had* been a beautiful day—until this man brought storm clouds rolling in.

The blue of his shirt brought out the sexy blue of his eyes, making him look appealing in a brash, heart-stopping sort of way. Not that Holly found him so, but some women would.

Most any woman, she amended, having to be honest.

"Can I interest you in a test drive, Mr. Murdock?" she asked him sweetly.

He twirled his sunglasses in a circle. "I noticed you had a profitable day. Are you trying to rub it in?"

She shot him a smile. "What's the matter, Jack—your big new sign failing you?"

"Not in the least. I just didn't have the volume you did. Anyone can have an off day."

Anyone who couldn't keep his eyes off Holly, Jack realized. He'd watched her trim little backside sashay around those cars of hers until his baby-blues were bloodshot. No wonder his customers didn't buy.

His heart wasn't in it today.

"Actually, I came over to offer *you* a test drive."

She raised one pretty eyebrow at that. "And why would I want to take a ride in one of those lame bucket of bolts you sell?"

"My cars are in good shape. Don't forget, I have Luther," he said and watched the fire spark in her green eyes.

"I haven't forgotten," she replied tightly.

"As a matter of fact, he's doing the final tune-up on my newest acquisition right now—a vintage red MG with wire wheels and black leather seats. A convertible. Should be ready for that test drive by tomorrow. But if you don't want to try her out . . ."

27

He wasn't above a little bribery. Not when it came to Holly. He'd never had to dangle temptation in front of a woman to get a date before, but then he'd never dealt with Holly Hanford before. The woman wasn't exactly fond of him.

Her eyes narrowed. "A red MG? Where did you get it?"

Vintage cars were Holly's passion. She knew every serious collector in the state, and she was certain none of them had a car like that that they'd turn loose.

He smiled and parked his sunglasses back on his handsome nose, leaving her unable to read his eyes. "A lady came in a few weeks ago—"

"Aha—I thought so."

"Thought so what?"

"You conned some unsuspecting soul out of that car—and a female at that. You worked your charm on her."

"My charm?" One eyebrow rose. "You think I have charm, Hanford?"

Holly crossed her arms and tapped the toe of her right foot.

"We were talking about the car."

"Ah, yes. The MG, the *red* MG. In spite of what you think, I offered her an honest price for it."

Holly pursed her lips, not knowing whether she believed his story or not. "So, is it in good condition?" she asked, deciding to give him a little more rope—in the vain hope he'd hang himself with it.

"Beautiful—inside and out—except for a frozen clutch, which Luther is repairing as we speak."

"Ah—yes. Luther." It still rankled her that he'd stolen Luther right out from under her nose. "And you're offering me a chance to drive it?"

Rub her nose in the fact that he had the little trophy and

she didn't, was more like it, she thought.

"Why don't I pick you up at two tomorrow?" he asked with a pleased smile on his face.

Tomorrow was Sunday—her day off—and she wasn't exactly thrilled to spend her afternoon with Jack Murdock. But she did want a chance to see that car, run her hands over its smooth lines, put it through its paces.

"Okay, Jack—two o'clock," she said and gave him directions to her house.

Holly was certain she'd lost her mind. She'd just made a date with Jack Murdock, a man about as trustworthy as a three-dollar bill.

She glanced across the street, searching for sight of the red MG, but she didn't see it. Luther was no doubt working on it as Jack had said. Well, she'd see it on Sunday.

The only problem was that Jack came with the day.

"What did Murdock want?" T.R. said, coming up behind her.

Holly nearly jumped a foot. Her thoughts had been on the little red car—and Jack. "He said he has an MG convertible and wants me to test drive it tomorrow," she said, dragging her gaze back from across the street.

"Does *he* come with this test drive?"

Holly avoided looking up into T.R.'s too-knowing eyes. The man could be like an overprotective parent at times, though in this instance Holly could no doubt use a little cautionary influence.

"Unfortunately he does, T.R."

But Holly intended to be careful. Jack was a man who could steal the fillings right out of her teeth.

Or worse, her good sense.

She gave his car lot one final glance, then her own. She still had customers who were looking—and she needed to keep her mind on business. With one final sigh at her idiocy where Jack was concerned she headed off to sell a few more cars before the day was done.

Jack closed up the lot a little early. His business was doing all right—or at least better than he'd hoped for this early in the game.

He'd come here a few months before, intending to buy himself a ranch, settle back and take life easy for a while. He'd made enough money from his job on Wall Street that he could afford that luxury, decide where he wanted to go next, what he wanted to involve himself in.

Jack never liked to stick around any one place very long. He supposed, considering that, buying the ranch had been a foolish move, but then he could always consider it an investment, make a tidy little profit from it like he intended to do with Mad Jack's.

Mad Jack's. Buying up a failing used car lot had been the last thing on his mind when he'd come here, but Jack never could resist a good deal. And old Pete Walters' lightly inventoried small business on the outskirts of McCallum had been a good deal. Pete wanted to leave town and was pleased when Jack came along.

One week after taking over, though, Jack knew that if he didn't want to go the way of the previous owner, he needed a better location for his business. He'd studied his competition, learned who the players were in this little burg and settled his newly acquired company smack-dab across the street from Hanford Motors. Holly's place was high visibility. She had a big clientele. And Jack intended to snare a few of her customers.

Life was good. Not perfect—but good. Then he remembered the date he had with Holly Hanford tomorrow afternoon. Maybe life was more perfect than he thought.

There was still activity across the street at her place. She probably wanted to get that very last sale. Jack wasn't quite that dedicated. Oh, he liked to make money all right—but he had a few other priorities. Like enjoying life along the way.

Holly took work way too seriously.

She was still annoyed that he'd moved in on her territory—but a little competition was good for business, Jack always felt. Besides, Holly would do well—she had good cars, a healthy sales staff, and the brains to make it all work.

He added the last of the day's sales figures into the computer on his battered old desk, hit save, then clicked his way out of the program and shut the thing down.

He made his way out onto the lot, locked up his own black SUV, which he was leaving here tonight, and jangled the keys to the red MG in his hand. Luther had finished the work on it as promised. And tomorrow he intended to make Holly drool over the gorgeous little car.

Chapter Three

Holly adjusted the pink-visored hat on her head and surveyed her appearance in the cheval mirror one last time. She refused to admit she'd taken any more pains dressing today than she did any other day.

Not for a date with Jack.

Check that: this was not a date.

Not anything of the sort.

She pirouetted to see the back of her pink madras shorts. *Too tight?* she wondered, for the umpteenth time. Before she could decide, the doorbell rang.

Jack!

She raced to the dormer window of her front upstairs bedroom. She wanted a glimpse of that car. Tugging aside the white lacy curtain she gaped openly. The little red car was an unqualified beauty, with a streamlined body, wire wheels and a shiny chrome grill.

A convertible—just as Jack had promised.

The doorbell rang again—this time with more insistence. Giving the car one final glance, she let the curtain slip back into place and headed down the stairs.

The little gem parked in her driveway had put her in a good mood.

She could even be nice to Jack Murdock.

Maybe.

She pulled open the front door and her breath caught as she looked up at him. His dark hair was wind-tousled from his ride and his tanned face glowed. The smell of fresh outdoors and spring sunshine clung to him. His faded jeans and black polo shirt accentuated the sinewy hardness of his body.

She tried to conjure up the eggplant-colored jacket with her mind's eye, but failed miserably. All she saw was Jack standing there, taking up space on her front porch, looking totally male and pleased with himself.

Jack liked what he saw as his gaze swept over Holly in those snug plaid shorts and pink sweater. Out of her Boss Lady clothes she looked even sexier, he decided.

Definitely sexier.

From beneath the cap shading her eyes, her hair tumbled to her shoulders. He could hardly wait to see those rich strands dancing in the wind, blowing across her pink cheeks and that dewy-fresh mouth of hers. "Ready to give this baby a spin, Hanford?" he asked.

She pursed her mouth in that delightful way she had. "I'll force myself."

She wasn't fooling him; she was just itching for a ride in that car of his—and he intended to dangle the enticing carrot in front of her for as long as it took.

"Oh, I almost forgot." He dragged a strand of his fake pearls from his pants pocket and slipped them around her neck. "Something special I always give the ladies for test driving one of my autos," he said.

She lifted the fake pearls and gave them an examining glance, then rubbed the beads over her pretty white teeth. "Ah—the real thing, I see. You're first class, Jack. I'll bet the ladies are just lining up to get a string of these."

33

"No need to be snide, Hanford. You want that ride or not?"

Holly did—and she could even endure Jack Murdock, much as she disliked his sneaky ways. "Let's go, Jack."

She made a lunge for the keys, but he held them high. "I'll drive for now. You'll get your chance later."

"Okay—have it your way, Jack." Holly wanted to drive—and badly, but for now she'd force herself to be content to ride.

He opened the passenger door for her and she slid in, letting the aged leather envelop her. The upholstery was in remarkably good condition for the age of the car. The whole interior was, in fact.

And if Luther had checked out everything under the hood . . .

Holly leaned back in her seat and let the wind whip through her hair as Jack raced along the parkway. The car had a style all its own. Like a beauty queen whose looks refused to fade with time.

"What do you think of her?" he asked over the sweet sound of the engine.

"I'll let you know *after* I get my chance to drive."

He let out a low, throaty chuckle that vibrated through her like the early rumblings of a Texas thunderstorm. "Just hold your horses, Hanford. You'll get your turn soon enough."

She daggered a glance in his direction. The man was a pain in the backside. Maybe spending the afternoon with him wasn't such a good idea, after all.

Except for the MG.

It was the reason she was here, she reminded herself.

He made his way through the Sunday afternoon traffic with ease, thoroughly enjoying the car and making Holly doubt he had any intention of ever letting her take the wheel.

She tapped her fingers restively on the dash, then quickly stilled them.

It wouldn't do to let Jack know he could rile her.

Finally, when they'd left the outskirts of town behind them, Jack pulled over to the side of the road. "Okay, think you can handle this baby without putting a dent in her fender?"

Holly groaned. "Jack—I *know* how to drive."

She quickly moved to change places with him, sliding into the driver's seat. It took her a moment to adjust the mirrors, then she put the little MG into gear and eased back into the parkway traffic.

The car drove like a dream, cornering well on the curves and doing great on the straightaway. It should belong to someone who would appreciate it. Someone like *her*.

Not Jack Murdock.

"I, uh, might consider making you an offer for the car," she said with an attempt at casual indifference. "After I have my mechanic look it over, that is."

He gave her a wily smile. Holly noticed it. This would not be an easy negotiation. Not with Jack. He flicked an imaginary piece of lint from his denim-clad leg, as if carefully considering her words.

She waited.

"An offer, huh . . . ?"

"Providing the price is right."

"Well, I'd have to think about that," he drawled finally.

It was the cat playing with the mouse, and Holly didn't like it. She'd always been able to play the game with the best of them, but she just might have met her match with this man.

"Don't wait too long," she warned. "I may not be in the mood later." It was an idle threat, and she was certain he knew it. Still, she had to try. She tromped down on the accel-

35

erator, ending their conversation.

Jack watched the lady's profile as they flew over the country roads. She wasn't fooling him. She wanted this car—and badly. He might consider selling it to her, but not just yet. As long as he had something she wanted, she'd keep coming back until she got it. He wished it was his unvirtuous body she lusted after—but the car would have to do for now.

"Turn right—onto the highway," he told her.

She gave him a puzzled glance. "Why?"

"It's my car, remember? I get to choose the route."

She gave him a look that could cut a lesser man down to size, but she made the turn, though it was on two wheels—and threatened to toss him out onto the shoulder.

"Take it easy," he warned. "I'd like to keep this baby in one piece."

"What's the matter, Jack—can't take the heat?"

He wasn't sure he could—at least not the heat Holly put out. "Just keep the car on the road, okay?"

She gave him a superior smile—but at least she knocked off the race car maneuvers. After a few miles the gates of big Texas ranches punctuated their route, each entrance more impressive than the previous.

Until they came to his small place.

At the moment the spread wasn't giving him much of a return on his money. Neither was Mad Jack's. But he wasn't worried. Jack had that Midas touch when it came to turning a profit.

In the meantime he'd work hard to turn the place into something a man could be proud of. An Easterner who'd cut his financial teeth on Wall Street could run a ranch as well as a native Texan once he got the hang of it, Jack was convinced.

"Turn here," he told her when they reached the entrance.

He wasn't sure why he wanted her to see the ranch. Maybe it was to show her there was more to Jack Murdock than a few used cars.

Or maybe he just enjoyed having her all to himself—at least for the afternoon.

"Where are we going?" she asked as she made the turn.

"To my place," he said.

"Your place?"

"Don't worry, Hanford. Your virtue is safe with me. I'm just going to show you around."

"Well, that's a relief."

Did he see a tiny hint of disappointment in her pretty face? Or was that his own wishful thinking?

Jack didn't know.

Just then a sprawling old ranch house came into view. Holly pulled the MG to a stop in front of it and cut the engine. She turned to Jack with stunned surprise. "This is where you live?"

She'd never really thought about Jack's lodgings before, but if she had, she'd have pictured two frightful rooms behind the car lot, not this large, inviting place.

"I gather from the gape of that pretty mouth of yours you thought I lived under a piece of cardboard in a back alley somewhere."

"Nothing that grand, Jack."

He gave her an amused grin. "Come on, Hanford, I'll show you the stables first."

Holly stepped out of the car and headed for the long, once-red building, all-too-aware of the man beside her, the muscles of his thighs flexing beneath the tight denim of his jeans, the power in his arm swinging so close to her own. She tried to blot out the raw heat of him, the scent of fresh out-

Gayle Kasper

doors in his hair. He seemed to fit this setting of hard earth, blue sky and rugged prairie.

Unlike the big rambling ranch house, the stables were a little worse for wear, however. Boards were missing in more than a few places and the roof looked as if it might blow away in the first stiff breeze that came along. Still, it wasn't unfixable—*if* Jack had the ambition to do the job. Unfortunately, the only ambition the man seemed to have at the moment was the desire to send Hanford Motors into red ink.

She tried to banish that dire thought from her mind as she looked inside the stables. The interior of it was dim and cool. The scent of hay and horses permeated the air, but all the stalls were empty. "No horses?" she asked him.

"Not yet," he answered. "The stables still need a lot of work and I haven't had the time to do the repairs."

She glanced over at him, her eyes narrowed. "Maybe you'd have the time if you didn't spend so much of it trying to put me out of business."

His sexy mouth quirked slightly. "Ah, now, Hanford, why would I want to do that? I wouldn't have any fun at all without you across the street."

"You're warped, Jack."

She heard his low chuckle as she stepped inside. Daylight filtered in through the sides of the stables and down through the holes in the roof, casting sunlight and shadows. Above she glimpsed an old hayloft with plenty of hay for those horses he intended to buy—*when* he tired of causing trouble for her and her company.

In one of the empty horse stalls she noticed a hammock strung between the two partitions. Holly had a quick mental image of Jack's male-hard body stretched out in it in total indolence. "I suppose this is where you plot your next move against me?"

38

He glanced over at the low-slung swing and ran a hand over his square jaw. "I suppose that could be one use for it."

"You have another?"

"Yeah, getting you into it, Hanford."

Holly gave a small gasp. The thought was all too vivid for her—and she forced herself to banish it from her mind. She didn't want to think of herself and Jack doing *anything* together in a hammock. "You're dreaming, Jack," she said.

"Maybe—maybe not."

She folded her arms in front of her. "And just what is that supposed to mean?"

His smile was slow and sexy as he fixed it on her. "It means that maybe you're not as unwilling as you like to think you are."

Holly was ready to clobber the man.

Maybe because he'd hit too close to the truth?

Why did she have to find Jack the least bit attractive? Why couldn't she just picture him in one of his wild jackets—the ugliest one? She started toward the stable doors, needing to air out her brain and put some distance between her and their annoying conversation.

Jack caught up with her as she emerged into the bright sunlight. "C'mon," he said. "I'll show you the house."

Holly wasn't sure a tour of Jack's personal space was a sound idea right now. *If ever.* It was safer to see him as the irritating rival he was.

"I have to get back," she said. "I've got some sales figures to go over tonight—and an ad layout to approve."

"An ad layout?" He jumped on that bit of news like a lemur. "How big an ad?"

"Now, why would I tell you? You'd just take out one twice the size."

He gave a low, sexy chuckle. "You don't have to worry

39

about me, Hanford. I may be your competition but I'm not out to wreck your business. Besides, I'm planning a TV commercial."

"Now I feel relieved," she replied tartly. "What do you intend to do? Sit up there on your roof until you sell some insane number of cars?"

"No—but now that you mention it, that's not such a bad idea."

Holly rolled her eyes.

He teased at a curl that fluttered at her cheek. "Why are you always so ready to think the worst of me?" he asked.

His touch was electric and it galvanized her to the spot. Jack Murdock was quicksand—and Holly didn't intend to sink into it.

"Because I don't trust you as far as the end of my elbow, that's why."

"Ah, now, Hanford, have I given you any reason to mistrust me?"

"Let's see, there's the mechanic you stole away from me; the little business of you usurping my territory with your dilapidated, bottom-end, used cars; that mortifying, oversized, ugly sign of yours—shall I go on?"

"Do you know how beautiful you look when you're angry?"

"I suppose you're going to tell me?"

"No—I'm going to kiss you."

Before Holly could fathom an objection he lowered his head. She forced her body to move, but it was doing its best to betray her. His fresh breath fanned her face. And then he stole from her what she didn't want to give him—a kiss, her peace of mind.

Her sanity.

His mouth brushed hers, lightly at first, then with more intensity. And she insanely kissed him back. She hadn't wanted to, certainly didn't intend to, but his kiss was so delicious, so heart-jolting, so mind-numbing that she couldn't help herself.

He nipped her lower lip, then lathed it with his tongue. Heat raced through her veins and ignited her every nerve ending. She needed to stop this.

This was Jack.

A danger to any female walking.

And she was kissing him back like a sex-starved woman.

"Jack Murdock, I don't intend to let you take advantage of me," she said when she could catch her breath, clearing the fuzziness from her brain.

She felt his smile against her lips. "Take advantage of you? Now, why would I want to do a thing like that?"

"Because you're rotten, Jack."

"Ah, now, Hanford, how can you say that?"

Before she could answer him he kissed her again. Her knees buckled beneath her. If she hadn't been leaning against him, she'd have fallen in a heap at his feet.

Jack had promised himself he wouldn't do this, that he'd keep hands off—but damn, self-control expected just too much of a man. Holly was so enticing, her mouth incredible, her kiss just the far side of sweet, quickly edging toward sultry.

How many nights had he dreamed of a taste of her?

But whatever his dreams had been, they couldn't match up to the reality. Holly was pure temptation, her mouth hot silk.

He'd like to have her on her back in that hammock in the stables—but he knew better than to press his luck. This was Holly—and she'd soon have big regrets. In fact, he'd be lucky if she didn't drop kick his backside into the next county.

She drew away, a little breathless, a lot shaken. And the look on her face wasn't pleased. "For the sake of business, Jack, I think we should forget that kiss ever happened."

Her green eyes had tiny gold flecks in them. Jack hadn't noticed that until now. Maybe it was the sunshine—or maybe he'd just been busy noticing *other* things about her.

Those other things didn't miss his notice now, either—her cool stature, those long gorgeous legs, her small firm breasts, his strand of fake pearls falling softly between their fullness, those lips that had haunted his dreams.

He brushed her lower lip with the tip of his finger. "Sure, Hanford," he said. "I will, if you will."

He could wait for another kiss. He wouldn't like it, but he could wait. He had the time; he had the patience.

And he had the red MG she wanted.

Chapter Four

Holly chose to drive on the way back to town. She needed to feel in control of something, though she suspected that where Jack was concerned, she was far from being in control of anything. And it was not a feeling she liked.

She'd *enjoyed* kissing Jack—which proved just how heavily in doubt her sanity really was. Her cheeks flamed at the memory. This was Jack—the enemy. He'd tempted her with one little red car and that sexy mouth of his. But not again.

From now on, she would be on her guard against him. He was history, as were their kisses. She liked her life just the way it was—no, the way it *had been*. Before Jack moved in on her territory and made it a nightmare.

She didn't need the man and his steamy kisses confusing her.

Holly was still cursing her stupidity—and vowing abstinence from anyone even *remotely* male—when she heard the whine of a siren behind her.

She darted a glance into the rearview mirror, then groaned loudly. Hot on her bumper, red lights whirling, siren at full wail was a police cruiser.

She shot a quick glance at Jack who daggered a look behind them, then fastened accusing eyes on her. "Okay, lead foot," he said, "just how fast were you going?"

"*Under* the speed limit—and thanks a lot for your vote of confidence, Jack."

She steered the car to the side of the road and fumed indignantly as the cop car pulled up behind them. She'd done nothing wrong—with the major exception of taking this joy-ride, joy-*less*-ride, with Jack Murdock. And—of course—kissing him like a wanton fool back there at his ranch.

What had gotten into her, anyway?

She shoved the thought aside as an even worse reality struck her. She shot a glower at Jack. "Is this a hot car? It *is*, isn't it?" If it was, she intended to wring Jack's neck right here in front of the cop.

"Now, Countess, how can you think that—?"

"Don't Countess me, you . . . you . . . *crook*."

"I hate to disappoint you, sweetheart, but the car isn't hot. I bought it—lock, stock, and hubcaps. I'll even show you the paperwork." He popped open the tiny glove box in the dash—but there wasn't as much as a lint ball inside. Strangulation was too good for him. Torture was better. Long, slow torture.

And she would enjoy it, too.

"Howdy there, folks."

Holly gave a low groan and slid down in her seat at the cop's greeting, wondering why she'd ever agreed to this afternoon with Jack. She knew he was trouble, knew she needed to keep her distance from him, romantically and every other way. Still he'd cajoled her into spending the afternoon with him, test driving the red MG.

The *hot* MG.

"Good afternoon, Officer," Jack said with all his male charm—which wasn't worth a great deal at the moment, Holly was sure. "I know it looked like the lady was going to a fire, but—"

44

Holly shot Jack an evil glance. She needed to kill him. *Now.*

"Sorry, folks," the cop returned. "You've got it wrong. No one was speeding."

Holly smiled, first at the nice officer, then over at Jack. No one was speeding, that should show Jack, she thought smugly. Then she thought again. If the offense wasn't speeding, it was . . . *grand theft auto.*

And she was the one behind the wheel.

"Uh, Officer, this isn't my car," she tried to explain hastily. She wasn't going to take the heat for Jack Murdock. The man could rot in jail for all she cared.

But the cop was busy inspecting the MG's gleaming chassis and kicking its tires as if he were a man deliberating a buy. Holly swallowed hard as he returned to her side of the car.

"Well, then," he said, "if the car isn't yours, whose is it?"

"Shady Jack's." She hooked a thumb in Jack's direction. "Confess now," she hissed under her breath at him. "Or I'm going to have to kill you."

If the man were a gentleman he'd get her out of this mess.

"Look, Officer, just what is the charge here?" Jack asked— as if he were Mr. Blameless.

"Charge? There's no charge. I just pulled you over to get a better look at this little buggy. She's a real little beauty, she is."

Holly stared up at the cop in astonishment. That was why he'd stopped them? The guy was a car buff who just wanted a look at the MG? No arrest for auto theft? No trip to the pen?

She glanced over at Jack, who was wearing a smug smile.

"Apologies are now being accepted, Countess."

Holly would sooner eat dirt.

It had been nearly a week since Holly had seen Jack, except for a quick glimpse of him across the street. The red MG, polished until it gleamed, sat in the front row on his lot where she couldn't miss seeing it every day. He knew that she wanted it—and he was tempting her with it.

Holly should put the man—and the car—out of her mind and run her business as if he didn't exist across the street, as if he weren't about to rob her of customers *and* her sanity. But all she could think about was that blatant charm of his—and the TV commercials he intended to run.

What would the TV spots do to Hanford Motors? How much business would he steal away from her? Jack claimed the competition would be good for them both—but Holly couldn't help but believe she'd have been much better off being the only game in this small strip of commercial domain. She'd run her business that way for the past two years, happy not having any competitive neighbor to make life difficult for her.

She knew, too, that she should forget that day she'd spent with Jack. She should forget the way the man could kiss, setting her senses on fire and robbing her mind of its good sense.

She snapped the blinds at the front office window closed so she didn't have to see the man, or his establishment, across the street. She had work to do and she didn't need reminders of Jack interfering with the run of business.

The ad campaign she'd launched in the newspaper had come out two days ago—a nice spread, she had to admit. It had brought in the customers and she'd been delighted with the increase in sales.

Maybe she didn't have anything to worry about from Jack—except for the way he could make the blood pound in her veins and her heart flutter like some silly schoolgirl's whenever he was around.

She hadn't forgotten the way he'd kissed her, the way *she'd* kissed him back. She'd never had a man steal away her good sense so easily, jangle her nerves, turn her to putty. If the kiss had gone on . . .

But Holly didn't dare think of that. Jack Murdock had already caused her enough headaches to last a lifetime.

She pushed away all thoughts of him and picked up her phone messages, absently thumbing through them. There was one from Brewer. She'd heard from him nearly every day since his retirement and she was glad he was still very much a part of her life.

There was another from her friend Leah, wanting to try lunch that noon at a new restaurant she thought Holly would like. Holly glanced at her watch and thought it would be nice to fit that into her day. Leah was a good friend, and Holly didn't spend much time these days keeping up with old friends.

The last message puzzled her. It was from a Mr. Eberhardt, with the firm of Eberhardt, Jones and Sullivan, a big law firm in town. She started to set the message aside then decided she'd make the call before she returned the one to Leah about lunch.

She was put through immediately.

"Ms. Hanford, I'm pleased you returned my call." The man's voice was professional and friendly. There was no reason to sense trouble, yet Holly did.

"What can I do for you, Mr. Eberhardt?" Maybe he was looking for a good used car for a family member, a son or daughter, a grandson . . .

"I think it's more what I can do for you," the man returned.

"And what is that?" Holly asked.

"I have a client who's interested in making you a generous offer for your business," he explained. "I wonder if

47

we might set up a time to meet."

It took Holly a moment to assimilate this. "If you're refer-ring to Hanford Motors, I'm not interested in selling, Mr. Eberhardt. You'd be wasting your time and mine."

"You haven't heard the offer," he returned.

Holly kept her voice even. "I don't have to. Hanford's is not for sale," she repeated.

"I think it might be if you knew the amount my client is willing to pay," he persisted.

"And who is this client?" she asked, suddenly aware the man wasn't going away as easily as she'd thought.

"I'm not at liberty to divulge that, I'm afraid. The bid is a silent one."

Holly was about to hang up, thinking this man had to be badly misinformed if he thought she was interested in selling her company—or that she would do business with anyone who hid anonymously behind an attorney.

Before she could do anything Mr. Eberhardt named a sum, one that was at least twice what her small lot was worth. Who would want Hanford Motors for that kind of money—and why?

Jack?

The possibility crossed her mind, and she couldn't ignore it. But was that really Jack's style? And why would he make such an offer when he could just as easily wait for her little company to fail because of his own lot's proximity?

"You may tell your client I'm not interested at any price, Mr. Eberhardt," Holly returned, this time brooking no argu-ment from the man.

She was trembling with anger when she hung up the phone.

She had no intention of selling out, not now, not ever—and she was irate to think someone, some *unknown* someone, could think that she would so easily give up what she'd worked so hard to achieve these past two years.

She hoped she'd heard the last from Mr. Eberhardt, but she doubted she had. His client sounded eager—and Mr. Eberhardt had obviously believed he could persuade her to listen to the insane offer, even to accept it.

Holly tried to calm herself, but she wasn't accomplishing the task. She picked up the phone to call Leah and accept her invitation to lunch, then replaced the receiver. She wouldn't be very good company today. Besides, she wasn't hungry, nor did she feel like catching up on old times with a friend.

She couldn't put the thought out of her mind that Jack could somehow be involved in this offer for her business. She wasn't at all sure what the man was up to, or just how far he would go to make his own business a success.

At her defeat.

Before she could contemplate Jack's guilt or innocence in it any further, there was a sharp rap on her office door. T.R. entered, his thick eyebrows furled into a frowning slant. "What is it, T.R.?" she asked.

"I thought you might want to know—your friend Jack Murdock is over there filming his commercial."

She opened her mouth to tell T.R. the man was not her friend, but it could wait. She wanted to see what was going on across the street.

"Don't tell me, let me guess. He's dressed as a cave man who's just invented the wheel. Or is it Majud the snake charmer? That's it, isn't it, the snake charmer?"

She could only hope the customers would think Mad Jack was truly mad when they saw his commercials and wouldn't come anywhere near his lot.

With a scowl, she started toward the front office window. The blinds were beginning to develop a permanent crook in the slats, but she had to see what Jack was up to.

She fully expected to find him dressed in a robe and turban, blowing on a flute or whatever it was snake charmers blew on. Maybe the cave man outfit. Even a gorilla suit wouldn't surprise her.

"He's going to ruin our business, T.R. The only advertising we do is the occasional newspaper ad. I can't afford to blitz the airwaves with thirty-second spots." Nor would she go to crazy lengths to attract potential buyers—not when she'd been doing just fine as she had been.

"We don't know it'll be a blitz, Holly," T.R. pointed out. "That takes money."

"It'll be a blitz. That man will be invading everyone's home in living color—the first thing in the morning, the last thing at night and with maddening frequency throughout the day."

T.R. didn't answer, just followed her to the window. A camera crew was busy setting up, and a crowd of onlookers had gathered to watch. Even the traffic along Woodland Avenue had slowed to a crawl as rubbernecking drivers surveyed the scene on Mad Jack's lot.

Then she saw the man in question. He wasn't dressed in a turban. He wasn't a cave man. He wasn't even a gorilla. That she might have been able to handle—but not this. Not Jack looking sexier than God intended any man to look, selling cars while sitting on the fender of the red MG.

The red MG she wanted.

On the other fender was a female model, with headlights on her Holly was certain weren't attainable by nature.

She gave the blond hussy only a cursory glance before her gaze returned to Jack. He was wearing an open-necked shirt with wide blue stripes that would make his eyes appear as honest blue as the sky and his smile as charismatic as a TV evangelist.

Why wasn't he wearing a gorilla suit, with his big, lurid sign winking behind him? Why wasn't he wearing one of his tasteless jackets? With this tantalizing look, the women would be tripping all over themselves to buy one of his cars.

Holly gave a low groan.

Jack thought the taping went well. The film crew had finally left. So had Miss Voluptuous January-through-December, and now he found himself at loose ends.

He hadn't seen Holly for almost a week, not since the Sunday they'd driven the little MG. Not since they'd shared those sultry kisses at the ranch. She'd been busy at work. He'd noticed more than a few smiling customers drive a car off her lot. It must have been that full-page ad she'd placed in the newspaper a few days ago.

Maybe he should have gone that way, too, instead of blasting a five-county area with TV commercials and a bosomy model. But the marketing people assured him this would get the most visibility.

Well, Miss Voluptuous was high visibility all right.

He paced around the lot, feeling the warm sun on his back, but his steps brought him to the MG. So far the car was just decorating his lot. He hadn't put a sales sticker on it, not because he didn't hope to sell it, but because the right customer for it was one beautiful woman across the street.

He still remembered the wind whipping through her silky dark strands as they'd driven out of town, her cheeks glowing from the created breeze and the warm afternoon sun.

Maybe he'd go over to see her now that everyone had left. He was feeling smug about his smooth business move.

Besides, he'd missed her.

51

He locked up his place—he hadn't had a single customer all day anyway—and made his way through the traffic racing along Woodland Avenue. T.R. greeted him with his usual gruff manner, but Jack ignored the man and headed straight for Holly's office.

She was there, seated behind her desk, looking beautiful. His breath caught in his throat and his heart hammered the backside of his ribs. What was it this woman did to him?

"Hello, Jack. What brings you over here on such a pretty day?" she asked, a half-smile tilting at her lips.

He angled a hip onto a corner of her desk. "I just came by to see if you noticed, um, all the activity at Mad Jack's this morning."

"Activity? As in . . . customers?"

She was playing coy. She couldn't have missed his filming venture. Half her sales staff had been watching. T.R. would have informed her; the man informed her of everything. "My commercial, Hanford. It took half the morning to film the thing. Don't tell me you didn't notice."

"Was that why those people were over there? I thought someone was actually going to buy a car. Better luck next time, Jack."

Jack chuckled. Holly was in true fighting form today—and he had to admit he was enjoying it. He liked a woman who could stand up to him, who gave as good as she got in any situation, and didn't let a man get a half inch ahead of her.

"The commercials will take care of that, I'm sure. Don't forget to turn on your television next week," he said. "The first one airs then—and I wouldn't want you to miss it."

"I'll be sure and fix popcorn."

Holly shoved the paperwork aside. She hadn't actually been working anyway. She'd just wanted to give Jack that impression. She stood up from behind her desk and paced a few steps away from it, hugging her arms to herself. She didn't know why she felt so defeated today. Or maybe she did. It was that phone call from the attorney—it was her suspicions that Jack was behind the offer he made to her.

She turned slowly and studied him intently, as if she could read deceit in his face, see it in his eyes. "Someone made me an offer for Hanford's this morning, a . . . generous offer."

"Why not," Jack said. "You've got a veritable gold mine here, Countess, a flourishing operation. Who wouldn't like to snap it up at any price?"

Inside, Holly's nerves clenched. Outside, not a muscle twitched. "So, it was you who made the offer. Are you out to buy up Hanford's for any amount of money?"

"Me? Buy Hanford's?" He gave a clipped laugh. "I can barely afford my commercials. Besides, this is *your* baby." He paused for a moment, then added, "Don't you know who made the offer?"

"No—I don't. The bid was a silent one, made through an attorney."

He quirked his sexy mouth at that, as if pondering the ramifications. Or maybe polishing his act. Holly couldn't be sure. If he was behind the offer, the act was a good one, she had to admit. In fact, she almost believed him.

Almost.

"Look, Hanford, that's not the way I do business. If I seriously wanted this place, I wouldn't beat around any legal bushes."

She let out a sigh and wished she knew whether to believe him or not. He could be innocent—or the one behind the anonymous offer.

This man knew all the right things to say, but she didn't know whether she could trust him. But there was one thing she *was* certain of however. Jack was trouble. She just didn't know in what way.

That evening Holly went home with a jackhammer of a headache. What had happened to her once-organized life? But she knew what had happened—Jack Murdock.

The man was going to be her downfall.

She pulled the Thunderbird into her driveway, turned off the engine and pressed her fingers to her throbbing temples, trying to rub away the pain. She had to get a grip on her life or Jack would soon be crowing with success.

And Holly would be deep in red ink.

Even if the man wasn't the one behind the offer for Hanford's, he was trouble aplenty—not only to her hormones, but to her sanity and peace of mind as well.

She gave an aggravated sigh and climbed out of the car. Maybe she'd string a big, wide banner over her lot to entice a few more customers in to buy.

A *tasteful* banner.

Taste was something Jack had in short supply.

She couldn't afford the TV advertising time, but maybe a two-page spread in the newspaper, not just the local paper, but the *Dallas Morning News*, as well. Yes, she'd consider that, she thought as she made her way into the house.

Whatever she did, she needed to keep a wary eye on Jack. He no doubt had something up his sleeve—besides one well-muscled arm and a string of sexy commercials.

Jack worked late on Mad Jack's lot that night, needing to finish up some paperwork. He had a few customers roll in, but they were mostly lookers. As soon as his commercials hit the airwaves, though, he'd be busier than a one-armed paper hanger, he knew. And he was looking forward to it.

He wished, though, that he had the spare cash to hire on more help—but he didn't. When he'd bought the car lot he'd jumped in with both feet, not giving much thought to the long term of it. Certainly not the way Holly planned out her business—down to every last detail.

He gave a curious glance across the street. Her lot was closed up tight. At least tonight she wasn't burning the midnight oil. She worked too many hours as it was, determined to keep a tight rein on her small company.

He thought about what she'd told him earlier today, about the call from the attorney and the mysterious buyer. Of course, she'd accused Jack of somehow being involved—but then, she accused Jack of everything these days.

He was innocent though. He didn't have the money to buy her out. Nor did he want to. He liked having her close by, liked the competition—and all the tangling and wrangling they did.

Still there was something funny about the call from the lawyer, something that didn't quite add up in Jack's mind. Why would a prospective buyer need to hide behind legal means?

Jack hoped Holly wouldn't consider the offer and sell out. He liked having her across the street, bedeviling the hell out of him, giving him a hard time, keeping him on his toes. He also liked watching her sashay around those cars on her lot. She was a beauty—and sexy as all get out. Without that gorgeous shape of hers around, what would he do for scenery?

He thought of the women he'd dated in the past—tall, cool and New York savvy. But he couldn't think of one woman who could hold a candle to Holly Hanford.

He hadn't forgotten the taste of her kiss, those silky warm lips of hers that had turned sultry-hot under his. He wanted to taste them again. He wanted to taste them often. Damn—

but he'd never known a woman who could send him into such a tailspin.

He finished up the paperwork on his desk. When his commercials aired he'd be busy on the lot. His cars were ready. Despite the fact that Holly called them clunkers, derelict hunks of tin and a few other unsavory designations, they were all in great shape. Luther had them up and running beautifully, and Jack had polished and spit-shined them until they gleamed.

Holly was just in a snit because he had Luther and she didn't. Nope, *snit* was too mild a word. *Hopping mad* was more apropos of her mood when it came to Luther. But business was business after all.

Though Holly didn't see it that way.

Jack gave a low chuckle. The woman was a jewel who'd stand out in a bag of gems. And she was his. Well, maybe not yet. But Jack could hope.

He locked up the office, realizing it was already dark out. He'd hoped to get some work done on the ranch before daylight waned—but it was too late now. A heap of hard physical labor might have gotten Holly off his mind long enough for him to get a good night's sleep for a change. Instead she'd have him tossing and turning half the night, his dreams haunted by the taste of her lips, her touch, her smile.

He gave a low groan and headed out to the MG.

Chapter Five

It hadn't taken long for Jack's commercials to air, or for the crowds to flock to his lot to see what he had to offer. Holly knew exactly what the man had to offer, one sexy body, oozing with male charm and sneaky tricks.

Tricks he wouldn't hesitate to use if it gave him an edge over her.

Holly frowned through her office blinds as she spotted Jack, that abundant male charm of his very much in evidence. He looked gorgeous; she hated to admit, dressed in tan chinos and a pale blue shirt. He even had on a tie for the occasion, the knot perfect, the color power-red.

He led a flock of his buying public around the lot, gesturing first at one auto and then another. Holly couldn't help but notice most of that buying public of his were women.

Had she expected otherwise?

She let the blinds snap back into place and got on the phone to her sales staff. T.R. answered. "That banner I ordered should be in sometime today," she told him. "When it arrives, string it front and center over the lot where it'll be highly visible."

"Does this have anything to do with Jack?" T.R. asked.

She squared her shoulders, though no one was there to observe her posturing. "It has to do with productivity for

Hanford's. Jack has nothing to do with this."

She crossed her fingers behind her back at the small white lie.

She needed to entice a few of those buyers of his over to her side of the street. How long, she wondered, would it take for them to realize that Jack was full of hot air instead of hot deals?

By the afternoon her staff had strung the sale banner high and wide as she'd asked them to do. It looked great over her lot, swaying to and fro in the warm Texas breeze.

Holly was pleased—that was, until the next day.

Saturday, the busiest day for business.

Jack had turned up the heat, with gaudy streamers flapping over his lot, big, bright balloons for all the kiddies, and a dozen long-stemmed red roses for all the women.

The new banner T.R. had raised over Hanford's had lured a few of Mad Jack's customers over to her side of the street— mostly men, who quickly saw through Jack's phony charm and who, no doubt, wouldn't let their wives or girlfriends go within a thousand feet of his place.

Something Holly should keep in mind when she was tempted to fall prey to the man herself.

She'd avoided watching his commercials, since the first one, when she'd hurled her high-heeled pump at the television screen and nearly followed that with her favorite antique lamp. The man had looked his sexiest, all hunky gorgeous male, alongside Miss . . . Headlights. It was enough to make any sane woman want to throw up.

But judging from the number of females she counted on his side of the street, there weren't many of those around this part of Texas. Where was the man's orange-plaid jacket when it could play to her advantage?

But Jack looked maddeningly handsome even wearing orange plaid, she remembered.

The week went by slowly for Holly as Jack's commercials continued to air, and the people continued to flock to his lot. Holly could only hope they weren't tempted to buy.

Friday evening, as Holly was ready to leave her office, Jack appeared in the doorway. He had on a pair of well-worn jeans that fit his hard body impressively, a soft white shirt—minus the power-red tie, this time—and a cocky smile on his all-too-handsome face.

"If you've come over here to gloat, Jack, just go away and take your sneaky bag of tricks with you," she ordered as she tucked some of her work into her briefcase and stood up behind her desk. She just wanted to go home and forget Jack Murdock at least for the night.

"I don't have a bag of tricks, sneaky or otherwise, Hanford. I'm just trying to do a little business. *Honest* business, I might add. Besides, I just came by to ask you for a date."

"I don't want a date. Now—go away." She snapped her briefcase closed and stepped out from behind her desk.

"Okay, have it your way." He shrugged his wide male shoulders. "I'll just invite someone else to go to the classic car auction with me this Sunday. My red MG is date bait, so I'm sure I can find someone to—"

"The classic car auction?" She paused and studied him seriously. "The one in Houston?"

"That's what I said. But if you don't want to go . . ."

Holly swallowed hard. "I didn't say that."

"Yeah, you did—I heard you clearly. And frankly, you hurt my feelings." He placed a hand over his heart as if she'd mortally wounded him.

"Your feelings are beyond pain, Jack Murdock."

The corners of his sexy mouth tipped upwards. "I

happen to have two preview tickets to the auction." He slipped the pair from his shirt pocket and waggled them in front of her.

The classic car auction was the buying opportunity of the year for aficionados. And the coveted preview tickets were as scarce as hood ornaments. They went only to the wheelers and dealers in Texas—which made Holly wonder just how Jack had managed to get his shifty hands on any. "I, uh, might consider going," she said.

He tucked the pair of tickets back into his shirt pocket and patted them—for effect, she was sure. "You might, huh?"

"Okay, Jack—yes, I'll go."

His smile broadened and Holly's worry level skyrocketed. What had she gotten herself into? Jack was trouble, more trouble than her traitorous hormones could handle—and that on a *good* day.

She should say no, back out now while she still could, but she needed to keep a wary eye on her competition, she reminded herself. She could not afford to let him outgun her.

Jack should feel guilty for tempting Holly into this date with him—but the woman didn't like him. What was any red-blooded male to do when confronted with a rejection from the woman he wanted to spend time with? And he wanted to spend time with Holly.

He knew when he was in trouble—and Holly was trouble in spades. Still, the beautiful spring morning was his to appreciate—and so was Holly. Even if she'd glared daggers at him when he'd picked her up.

"Did you forget your smile this morning, Hanford?" he asked.

Holly frowned over at him. "It wilts when you're around, Jack."

The woman was in perfect fighting form today, Jack had to admit. Maybe that was why she intrigued him the way she did—she was a worthy opponent. Her sass egged him on. And if she knew the power she had over him, he'd be history fast. But Jack was not about to let that happen.

The highway stretched out like a ribbon in front of them and the MG purred along beautifully. Luther had done a great job with the little car. He owed the guy. He felt another quiver of guilt for stealing the mechanic away from Holly. But business was business, after all.

All was fair in love and war.

Love . . . ? Jack would be far safer keeping it war between him and Holly Hanford, he knew, but he wasn't sure how long he could keep that up—not when the woman dazzled him the way she did.

He'd never met anyone like her before. He had to admit she wasn't really his type—but his body didn't want to agree with that small detail. Her short denim skirt had slid enticingly up her trim thighs. Jack hadn't missed the sight.

Nor had his unruly libido.

Her white blouse had dipped just low enough in front to get a man's imagination humming with randy thoughts. Her maple-brown hair whipped in the breeze, blowing across her ruby lips as they drove, lips he'd love to taste. And intended to—if luck was on his side today.

Trouble. This was where Jack got himself into trouble. Holly wasn't a woman out for a good time. She wouldn't tumble to just any man. She'd have her sights set on the long term.

Still she intrigued him.

"Did you bring your checkbook with you, Hanford?" he asked. "They should have lots of little charmers at the auction today."

61

She turned her head and her green-eyed gaze made his breath catch and his heart do crazy stunts in his chest. "Did *you*, Jack?"

"I sure did. Can't pass up any opportunity in this business."

Holly knew that was true. "I might be enticed to buy," she returned. "We'll see."

A short while later they stopped at a busy truck stop for a calorie-loaded breakfast. She watched Jack shovel in a huge order of biscuits and gravy and wondered how he kept that sexy body in shape with an appetite like that.

She let her gaze travel slowly over his mile-wide shoulders and trim waist until he glanced up and caught her frank perusal of him. Her face heated up and she looked away, fully expecting some smart remark from the man about her pleasure trip over his physique.

Instead he grinned—dangerously. "You're not eating your skinny-mini breakfast," he said. "Don't you like it?"

She'd been picking at her yogurt and granola, the only item on the menu that wouldn't put fifteen pounds on her just looking at it. "Stick to your plate of cholesterol—and don't worry about me." She took a spoonful of yogurt, not about to admit she'd been admiring the man's body. "I've just been considering my budget limitations for the auction."

Jack sobered a little at that. "Yeah," he said with a grimace, "budgets do put a damper on things in the car business."

Holly was surprised he understood that, that he appreciated the problem was part of what they dealt with on a weekly basis. She, and most dealers, operated on a very slim profit margin. Perhaps Jack had a canny business sense after all, that this wasn't all just fun and games to him.

Jack handed the preview tickets over to the man at the entrance and he and Holly stepped into a world of primo classic autos—most, he was sure, with price tags neither he nor Holly could afford. But there was always the chance of landing some cool little bargain he couldn't pass up.

Holly's eyes lit with excitement as she made her way along the first row of cars. Jack wished he could turn that excitement in *his* direction, that she would run those sweet hands of hers over *him* the way she was doing to the fender of that vintage silver Rolls she'd stopped to admire. It made him hot just thinking about it.

The preview showing would give them an advantage when the bidding began. They'd have a better idea of the car's proper value and condition. Jack was glad he'd gotten the tickets. He'd had to do some fast-talking to get his hands on any, but it was worth the trouble—the perfect bait to nudge Holly into this "date" with him.

If he could call it a date.

He'd do better keeping his mind on business and *off* the woman he was with.

There were several cars he wanted to bid on. A low bid, of course. He didn't have the cash to go into this in any real big way. He wondered if Holly would bid—and how high she might go. She'd stopped at a green MG with a bubble top, appraising it thoughtfully.

"My red one's snazzier," he said over her shoulder. A subtle whiff of her sexy fragrance wafted upward, turning his brain to mush.

"Somehow I knew you'd say that," she countered, continuing to appraise the little car in front of her.

From the looks of the exterior alone Jack suspected the green bubble top would take a ton of TLC to get it in shape. TLC—and money. He hoped Holly wasn't serious about bidding on it. He could see areas of rust on the body that looked like a honeycomb on steroids.

"You'd be better off buying my red one if you want one that badly—and don't forget, mine's a convertible," he wagered as she tried to pull open the stuck driver's side door.

"Trust me, Jack, I don't want one badly enough to deal with you."

Jack gave a slow grin at her remark. It was one of the many things he liked about her; she always had a stinging comeback to level at him. But he knew she wanted his little car. She'd practically drooled over it again today—though she was careful not to let him notice.

She was just biding her time; then she'd negotiate. And Jack would have to be careful he didn't get fleeced when she did. Holly was fair, but she could also drive a hard bargain.

And Jack was so infatuated with her; he could easily become a patsy for any fool deal she offered.

To his relief she moved on, leaving the green MG behind. Jack followed along, enjoying the view of her sexy backside as she moved down the row. Her lush brown hair swung in a silky veil, brushing her narrow shoulders. He liked it down, free and wispy. He also liked it up, revealing the slender column of her neck, giving him the itch to loosen it and sink his fingers in its richness.

Cars. He was supposed to be looking at cars. But his checkbook wasn't singing at anything he saw. Of course Holly had him deeply distracted.

She stopped to inspect the price on an old Edsel—a faded aquamarine number with high, wide tail fins that made it look like it could swim the Atlantic.

No way, his head screamed.

The car was ugly when it came out and it hadn't improved any with age.

"No, Countess," he whispered in her ear. "Move on—and

fast. That car's a behemoth and too unclassy for you."

She spun around and faced him. "And you are an authority on class, Jack?"

He gave a frown. "There's no need to get snarky, Hanford. I know ugly when I see it—and that car is *bone* ugly."

He took her by the hand and moved her down the row to a pretty little black Fiat, spit-polished until it gleamed. "Now this one's a *beaut*," he pronounced.

It was a buy that called out to his checkbook. He could almost hear the throaty rumble of the engine. And, as near as he could tell, it was in prime condition, too.

"Yeah, Jack, you need to buy this one. You—and a Swiss bank."

He didn't need to look at the starting bid Holly was scrutinizing. He knew it was top dollar—and most certainly not in his budget.

Still a man could dream.

He gave a dark sigh, then moved on. Holly trailed along behind, taking in one car and then another. The day was heating up. Jack was glad the bidding would take place in the large tent set up near the end of the rows of cars.

Holly, however, didn't seem to notice the temperature. She looked fresh as a garden daisy in spite of the sun's warm rays, as she checked out the autos.

Jack paused to inspect an old Buick laden with fifties' chrome, a buy that just might be in his price range. It needed a little work on its blue exterior. The upholstery wasn't the best, but it wasn't bad. It could be a work-in-progress, he thought, seriously considering the prospect.

He opened the driver's side door and slid in behind the wheel. "Hey, Hanford, think this one brings out the blue of my eyes?"

Holly did an eye roll.

Apparently she didn't think so.

He abandoned the Buick in search of something else.

Holly had started down another row by the time he caught up to her. "Change your mind about the Buick?" she asked.

He shrugged. "Wrong shade of blue."

"For your eyes?"

"Right."

She shook her head and moved on, checking out first one car and then another. Jack wondered what was going on in that shrewd brain of hers, which car tempted her to buy? Her expression was veiled. If she found a sweet deal, she'd never let him know it.

The woman was smart, as well as beautiful, he thought as he watched her operate on all six-cylinders. Jack's cylinders were on the blink whenever he got within ten feet of her.

Not a good omen for the day, he knew.

Holly raised her number, indicating her bid on the classy little cream-colored Karmann Ghia she'd spotted in the preview. It would be a great addition to her showroom of specialty cars and bring a fair profit when she sold it. Jack had been right about the green MG, though she hated to admit Jack could be right about anything.

The bid immediately rocketed higher and Holly spun around to see who her rival was. "Jack!" she screeched. "I want that car—and you're driving up the bidding."

"Oh, no—I want the Ghia. Besides, I saw it first."

"You did not—I did."

He frowned. "Didn't you see me kick the tires?"

Holly sighed in exasperation. "Since when does kicking the tires show proof of ownership? Proof of *anything?*"

The man was reprehensible. She raised her number again,

indicating she'd pay more than Mad Jack. How much more, she wasn't certain.

But if the man were a gentleman, he'd bow out.

Instead he topped her bid.

She whirled again in his direction. "Jack, I'm going to commit mayhem on that body of yours."

"Geez, Hanford, that sounds kind of kinky, but if you're into that stuff, I'm game."

Holly fixed him with a scorching glower and shoved her number in the air once more, then turned back to Jack. "Mayhem is *not* kinky sex," she hissed. "And if you had a brain at all you'd know that."

"I'm disappointed—I was beginning to *like* the idea of a little fun."

"Fun? Your idea of fun is besting the next guy."

"Not a guy—*you*, Hanford."

He raised his bid and Holly quickly raised hers higher. By this time she'd lost track of how much she was even bidding. Jack had put her off her game.

"Going once, going twice," the auctioneer called out.

"I want that car," she said, daring Jack to even flinch.

He didn't.

"Going three times. To the pretty little lady in the back of the tent," the auctioneer announced with finality.

Jack smiled. "Congratulations, Hanford—you just bought yourself a car for more than it was worth."

Mayhem was too good for him. "And whose fault is that, Jack? *You* drove up the bidding."

"I'm happy to be of service."

Holly turned her back on the man and strode over to the small office set up to handle the sales of the vintage cars. Jack was right about one thing—she'd just bought a car for more than it was worth. Damn the man. She should have let him have that final bid.

Maybe it would have put a dent in Mad Jack's finances.

She could still get a nice price for the Ghia, but the profit margin would be pretty slim—if there was any profit at all. She had to be more careful—too many foolish business mistakes like this one, and she could find herself financially poor.

Holly made arrangements to pick up the Ghia the following week. She'd send one of the men from her repair department with a flatbed to transport the car to Hanford's. More expense she didn't need to incur, she thought, and heaped evil curses on Jack's handsome head.

When she emerged from the building she glanced around for him and found him where she'd left him, watching the auction. "What's the matter, Jack, can't find anyone else's bid to drive up?"

"Don't get nasty, Hanford. I like you much better when you're just a tad sweeter."

"I didn't come along on this trip to be liked."

Jack watched as she stalked off in the opposite direction of the auction tent, that sassy little swing to her backside a mighty enjoyable view. He gave a low groan, picked up his pace and trekked after her.

"Through buying?" he asked when he'd caught up with her.

She spun around and stared him down. "Don't push my buttons, Jack. I'm just one step away from strangling you."

That's what he loved about Holly—all that fire and fury.

He'd had enough of the auction though. The bidding had gone too high for him to find any real deal out there. Besides, it was three o'clock and his breakfast had long since worn off. He needed sustenance—if he was going to keep on his mettle with Holly. "How about lunch?" he asked. "I'm hungry and I saw a nice little restaurant back out on the highway."

"I'm not hungry."

"Well, I am. And I'm the driver." He dangled the MG's keys in front of her.

The fight seemed to go out of her then—like a spent balloon. Her usually squared-for-battle shoulders gave an indifferent shrug. "Fine—I could use a tall iced tea."

"Atta girl."

She headed for the parking lot and the little MG. Maybe Jack had been too hard on her. He knew she was worried about her buy today. He felt a swift stab of guilt about bidding against her—and knew he needed to make amends.

He tried to engage her in conversation over their super-duper-sized burgers with everything, but Holly only shot him a frown no matter the subject.

She sipped her iced tea and barely nibbled at her burger with that sexy mouth of hers. He hadn't forgotten the taste of those warm, luscious lips and he wanted—needed—to taste them one more time. "Would it help to say I'm sorry?" he asked.

"No."

"Okay, I shouldn't have driven up your bid. Is that better?"

"No."

"That car will be a good addition to your showroom—and you know it. So maybe you paid a little over what someone else might have paid, but—"

"Shut up, Jack."

Her disposition didn't improve once they were back on the road and headed home, so Jack kept quiet for the first few miles. The day had heated up and didn't promise to cool down anytime soon. The convertible provided its own created breeze, however, so the ride wasn't uncomfortable.

Holly seemed to be silently ruminating about her questionable business deal. Actually it was a sweet little car. "I'll take the Ghia for what you paid for it," he offered. He'd bid on the vintage auto initially because he'd wanted it for Mad Jack's.

Her gaze shot to his. "*You* want the car?" Suspicion lit her eyes.

"Yeah—I bid on it in the first place because I wanted it, remember?"

She continued her wary stare, pinning him with those exotic emerald eyes of hers. "No."

"No—what?"

"No—you can't have it. If you want the Ghia—then it can't be the overpriced deal I thought it was. If I know one thing about you, Jack Murdock, it's that if there's a buck to be made, you'd take advantage of it. I like the car—and it's going in my showroom until I get the price I want for it."

Jack arched an eyebrow. "What's wrong with making a buck? Isn't that the idea of the game, Hanford?"

"There are a few other things than profit in this business. Like honesty, creating a good name for yourself and your company, *trust*."

She'd said the last like it was the most important to her. He recalled the vulnerability he saw in her face before—and he saw it again now. If a man dared abuse Holly's trust, God help the poor fool, Jack thought—and warned himself to be on guard.

He wanted to ask her about it, about her past, her reasons for that all-fired wariness of hers, wariness usually directed at him—though he'd seen it directed at others, too. But he doubted she'd welcome his questions—at least, not now.

That he would save for another time and place.

She'd turned her head, ignoring him, watching the passing

70

scenery instead—though scenery along the interstate didn't have much to offer. She was apparently done with her lecture to him.

Holly was a woman with passions. Jack just needed to change that passion from anger at him to something else—like a shared night of hot sex.

Just the thought heated the male blood in his tortured veins.

About a hundred miles northwest of the city, Jack decided to leave the interstate. The Texas byways were far more interesting, the traffic was usually lighter, and there were small roadside stops that the hurried drivers of today seldom saw.

"What are you doing?" she asked as he took the exit to the right.

"I thought it would be nice to see Texas from an alternate view—I'm tired of passing billboards."

She studied him intently, probably for some sign of skullduggery on his part. He really was going to have to work on that trust factor of hers. "Jack, I would like to get home *sometime* today."

"You will, Hanford, you will."

He whipped the MG onto the two-lane farm-to-market road, not exactly sure where it led—except that it was in the rough general direction of home.

They'd left the billboards behind with the interstate. The road curved through the countryside of flat plains, an occasional house and small towns he doubted had ever been seen on a map.

It was a far cry from New York City—that was certain. Jack didn't regret his move to Texas—especially with Holly in his life. Well, maybe she wasn't exactly in his life, at least not the way he'd like, but a man could hope.

They'd driven about sixty miles when the MG began to

cough and sputter. Jack checked the gauges. The tank was nearly full, the engine temperature normal, the oil gauge fine.

"What's wrong?" Holly's pretty forehead was pleated in a frown of worry and alarm.

"I think it's just a stutter in the engine. Probably nothing to worry about," he assured her, though he felt far from assured himself. "See, it's quit now. Want to stop for an ice cream in the next little town?"

Jack had barely gotten out the words when the engine coughed again—and died.

Chapter Six

Jack climbed out of the MG, and Holly was right behind him.

"I haven't had a guy pull this trick on me since high school, Jack Murdock," she fumed.

He spun around to face her. "What—stranding you along the road so he can make out with you? Well, guess again, sweetheart. This isn't a trick."

He released the hood latch and ducked his head under it. Holly gave a dispirited sigh as he jiggled the wires, no doubt searching for a loose one as the cause of their predicament.

She wished this *was* one of Jack's shady tricks.

She preferred making out with him to being stuck out here in the middle of nowhere. In fact, the thought sent a definite tingle through her veins.

"Do you know what you're looking for under there?"

That must have ticked him off. He straightened up, hit his head on the underside of the hood—and let out a colorful oath.

"Sorry," she said.

"You should be." He rubbed the back of his head and gave her a sharp glower before returning his attention back beneath the hood. He checked fluid levels, jiggled more wires and cursed even more.

Holly leaned against the fender and watched his tinkering.

She knew a lot about cars—unfortunately the inner workings of them she always left to her repair department.

After what seemed like forever, Jack's head re-emerged.

"Do you know what's wrong?" she asked.

"Yes—I know what's wrong."

"What?"

"The MG is deader than a carp."

That was not the answer Holly was looking for. She sighed. "Now what?"

"We can make out."

He drew her hard against him and Holly's tingle of a few moments before turned into a definite jolt. His chest was broad and solid. The top of her head came to just below his chin, and as she looked up, she saw heat darken his blue eyes.

"Jack Murdock, are you sure this isn't one of your shady tricks?" she said, giving his chest a quick push.

"I swear."

She narrowed her eyes at him, checking for signs of deceit. She wouldn't put anything past Jack. "Maybe we can call a road service," she suggested.

"Just what I was going to do." He flipped open his cell phone, his gaze sliding over her with more familiarity than she was comfortable with at the moment. Jack could make her pulses sing with very little trying.

She just hoped he came up with something to put them back on the road again—and soon.

She went around to her side of the MG, opened the door and sat down. She scanned the deserted highway for any sign of a passing tow truck—but not even a car came into view. Jack was still making calls and she thanked her lucky stars there were cell phone towers around even if there were no passing motorists.

Jack had coasted the car to the side of the road where an

old oak tree graciously shaded it. At least the temperature was *somewhat* more bearable under its sheltering branches.

Finally Jack finished his calls and came over to the shade beside her. "Did you find a tow service?" she asked hopefully.

"Nope. The closest tow was out on a call and it would be at least two hours before the guy could get here."

"Two hours?" Holly's heart sank and her shoulders with it.

"I knew you wouldn't be happy about that, so I made another try."

"And?" She felt a revived spurt of hope.

"I called Luther. He knows this part of the country and said he can be here in less than an hour. With his tools and expertise we should have the MG purring down the road again in no time."

Jack was right about that. She knew Luther's skills with recalcitrant cars. After all, he'd been *her* mechanic just a few weeks before.

Her feelings were a mixture of relief that Luther was on his way and renewed anger at Jack for stealing the man away from her in the first place.

The breeze stirred the leaves on the trees. The humidity had to be near a hundred percent this afternoon. And Holly's petulance raised it even higher. She dug in her purse for a hair clip, found one, and lifted her hair up off her neck, fastening it with the clip. "I sure could use a cold drink about now," she said. "You don't happen to know if there's any sort of a town within walking distance, do you?"

"Nope—but we don't have to walk. I have a cooler in the trunk."

That improved her mood in record time.

She could have kissed the man.

On second thought, that wasn't such a good idea. Her hormones were already on a short fuse around him. She didn't need to compound the problem.

Jack produced two chilled soda cans and a blanket from the trunk. "Sorry it's not wine, but this will have to do," he said.

Ice slid invitingly down the sides of the cans and Holly thought she'd never seen anything so gratifying in her life.

He looked around for a place to spread out the blanket. "Come on," he said. "There's a stream bed over that rise—*with shade.*"

Holly followed him up the hill. The spot looked serene and cool. The creek bed was strewn with smooth rocks. After a rain it would probably run full, but today, without a cloud in the sky, it was only a burbling stream. But she wasn't complaining.

The place was idyllic.

She helped Jack spread the blanket on the soft grass beside the water, then sank into its relative comfort. Jack popped the top on the soft drink cans and handed one to her.

Holly drank greedily, then sighed. "This is almost pleasant."

"Only *almost?*"

She gazed over at Jack. He looked somewhat cranky—probably because the MG had outwitted him. A male thing, she surmised.

"*Very* pleasant," she amended, glancing up at the tree boughs that shaded them from the treacherous sun.

"Still want to buy the MG, Hanford—it's at a rock bottom price right now."

"And as soon as it's up and running again, you'd just try to buy it back from me. No thanks, Jack. Besides, I just spent the last of my available cash on a Karmann Ghia, remember?"

He took a long, slow swallow of his drink. His throat muscles worked in his tanned neck and Holly couldn't tear away her gaze. Jack was too good-looking for her sanity right now.

She tried to focus on something beside Jack Murdock.

Like that cooling stream.

"As soon as I finish my drink, I'm going to dunk my feet in the water," she said.

That would be a sexy sight, Jack thought—then remembered his libido. It had been on fire being around Holly all day.

She'd tucked her hair up off her neck in deference to the heat and he wanted to plant a dozen kisses on that gorgeous column. He wanted to loosen the clip holding her hair and smile in awe as the strands tumbled to her shoulders.

He wanted to kiss her and feel her sweet body under him.

Damn, but he was in trouble here. Holly had had him on edge from the moment he'd picked her up today—and things weren't getting any better.

He took a long, hard swallow of his drink.

The chill cooled his throat but did little to cool his desire.

Holly was beautiful. Backlit by the setting sun, she sat prim and elegant, holding her drink as if it were champagne in a crystal flute. Her short denim skirt had ridden enticingly up her thighs and her white blouse outlined her firm breasts.

He hoped like hell Luther showed up soon.

"Tell me about Hanford's," he said, deciding conversation was safer than his edgy thoughts. *Business* conversation. Besides he wanted to know more about this woman who could scramble his senses.

"Why?" she asked—and he heard the note of wariness in her voice.

It was always there just below the surface, and he wondered about it, what had caused it—but he doubted Holly would tell him. She was too suspicious of his every action.

He leaned back on the blanket, his head propped on one

elbow. "I'm not asking for any corporate secrets here," he said. "I'm just . . . *curious*."

She seemed to relax a bit then. "What do you want to know?"

"Well, I know your dad started the business—and that you took it over after he died. I also heard about a few . . . uh . . . Saturday night poker games in Hanford's back room."

"How did you hear about that?" she asked, unable to hide the small smile that tilted at her lips.

"From . . . *sources*."

She narrowed her eyes at him, probably wondering just where he'd gotten his information—and what else he might know.

"Well, it was definitely the action in town back then, and my dad and Brewer often owned the other's lot—lock, stock and inventory—depending on the hand played on any given night."

Jack grinned at that. "Did you work there then?"

"No, though I wanted to. It wasn't any place for a woman, my dad thought. He believed a woman should be . . . *softer* somehow."

"Softer than Saturday night poker games played in back rooms?"

"Softer than being in the business at all. My parents packed me off to college for an English degree—a more *fitting* goal, in their words." She let out a breath and her voice dropped. "I was surprised when he left Hanford's to me."

"And you took it over two years ago?"

She nodded. "My dad had let things slide after my mom died. But I was determined to return it to the business it once was. I still am."

"You've done a great job with it, Holly."

She turned to Jack. "I don't like talking about me. Tell me

about you. All I know is you were some financial whiz on Wall Street."

He laughed. "I'm not so sure about the whiz part, but the job was fun—at least, for a while. New York is fast-paced, intense. Texas feels like a whole other world from that."

Holly could imagine. "Why did you start up Mad Jack's?"

"I bought up Pete Walter's old place, but I didn't like the location."

"So you moved it across the street from mine."

Pete Walter had never been competition for her—but Jack was a threat. To her senses. To her sanity. If not to her business.

"*That* was my smartest move, Hanford."

And *her* problem. "Do you have family in New York?"

"Nope—in Philly. Philadelphia. My mom and two sisters."

"Are they older? Younger?"

"One older, one younger. They're both married with a passel of kids for my mom to dote on. My dad died of a heart attack when I was sixteen."

"That's a hard age to lose a dad."

He nodded. "It was hard on all of us."

"How about girlfriends, ex-wives?"

Jack gave a slow grin. "Are you curious about me, Hanford?"

"I'm just . . . asking." The man did make her curious, but she didn't want to let him know that. It would send his male ego soaring.

"A few old girlfriends—but no trips to the altar. What about you?"

Holly had dated in high school and college, but no one seriously. Then there was Adam—but she didn't want to discuss him with Jack. "A few old boyfriends," she said, hoping that was the end of the conversation.

And it was.

A truck loaded with hay bales pulled to a stop on the road next to the MG. A weathered old cowboy rolled down his window. "Y'all need any help?" he hollered.

Jack stood up. "No, we're fine. Thank you." He waved the guy on and the truck lumbered on down the highway.

When he turned back, Holly had stepped out of her shoes and was headed for the creek. She tested the water with her pretty pink-painted toenails.

"Watch out for snakes."

She jerked her foot back and Jack had to laugh. Humor was better than thinking of those sexy painted toenails of hers.

"That wasn't funny, Jack."

She waded in, letting the water eddy around her ankles as she stepped gingerly over the stones. The creek's water ran clear as it headed to lower ground. Holly looked like a water nymph in the golden glow of the fading sunlight, a siren song that would steal his soul if he wasn't careful.

Just then her foot found a slippery place and she teetered precariously, trying to regain her balance.

"Holly!"

Jack splashed in after her, an attempt to catch her before she fell. She tumbled backwards into his arms, safe, but pure danger to his senses. She felt so soft, so pliant, so . . . sexy as he turned her in his arms.

"You didn't need to catch me. I wasn't going to fall."

"Yeah—*sure*."

With the way she fired up his libido he should have let her land on her pretty backside in the water. It would have been far safer.

Her lips were sweet and inviting, and so very close. The

water lapped around his pant legs and his favorite pair of western boots, but he barely noticed. It was the feel of Holly in his arms that held his attention. Those tempting curves, her soft, feminine scent.

He lowered his head and stole a kiss—something he'd wanted to do all day. Her lips parted on a sigh and his tongue sought the inner recesses of her sweet mouth. She was silk and fire. Her body relaxed against him, soft, yielding, his own body hot with dangerous need.

Damn, but she felt so good against him, like no other woman ever had before. At least none that he could remember. Right now all he could think about was Holly, sweet-scented, wonderfully feminine, wildly sexy Holly.

He wanted to go on kissing her, holding her. He wanted to make wild passionate love to her, but Holly wouldn't go for that, he knew. She barely tolerated him. Though, with the way she was kissing him back, he had a few doubts about that. She felt so damned good in his arms, her mouth, her kiss just this side of insanity. And Jack knew he could never get enough of her.

Her father hadn't wanted her in the business, believed a woman should be softer, he remembered her saying, but there was nothing harsh about Holly Hanford. She was soft in all the ways a woman should be soft.

And then some.

Holly knew she should stop this, pull away while she still could.

The man was addictive, his kisses dangerous.

His body was hard against hers, igniting crazy feelings she knew she shouldn't be feeling. Not with Jack. His hands went to her bottom, pulling her into his hardness. He wanted her; his body gave him away. And right now, this minute, she wanted him—the way she'd never wanted any man before.

Jack dragged out every womanly need she had and laid them bare. He took her breath away when he touched her, when he kissed her. He took her breath away even from across the street, when she just saw him walking across his lot. But that was something she had to get under control.

She didn't want a man in her life.

She *definitely* didn't want Jack in her life.

Just one more kiss, one more moment of this insanity, she thought, then she'd pull away and slap his handsome face for taking advantage of her.

And climb out of the creek.

But before she could do either, his hands slipped her blouse loose from her waistband and slid up her back—hot, dangerous, igniting every nerve ending she had. And she forgot her vow of a moment ago. His thumbs slid upward, touching the sensitive underside of her breasts and hot need exploded in her. The rough pads of those delightful thumbs abraded her nipples and fireworks went off. Holly sucked in a breath.

"You like that, sweetheart?" he asked, his voice low, throaty.

"Damn you, Jack Murdock."

"You want me to stop?"

"Yes. No."

"Okay, babe—which is it?"

She ought to kick him in the shins and run for safety, but her need for more held her prisoner. His lips found the sensitive nape of her neck and he planted dangerous kisses there, sending delicious shivers through her body. She trembled in his arms and he kept up the sweet torture, his thumbs still doing dangerous things to the nubs her nipples had become under his assault. Her breath came in short gasps. Her hands traced the hard muscles in his back, his lean waist, those male hips she wanted to drag closer to her femininity. How could this man drive her into such madness?

In the distance, somewhere beyond the haze of her need, she heard a vehicle. She worked to pull herself to consciousness. "Jack, I think we have company."

"They'll go away."

She turned to peek over his big wide shoulder. Company *had* arrived—in the form of Luther Anderson. The very man Jack Murdock had stolen away from her.

Back when she hated Jack for every sleazy, sneaky thing he ever did to her. Back before he'd kissed her and made her lose her sanity.

Reality re-emerged with an explosion.

She shoved him away in a gesture she couldn't have done a moment ago—not if her life depended on it.

"Jack Murdock, *your* mechanic is here."

At least Luther had the good grace to look sheepish. It was the first time she'd seen him since Jack had stolen him from her employ. Though the *full* blame for that she placed on Jack's sneaky head. And he was sneaky—after all, he'd just found a way to make her fall into his arms and kiss him like a wanton woman.

"Hello, Ms. Hanford," he said as he dragged his tools over to the lifeless MG.

"Good afternoon, Luther."

The man was nearing forty and a few gray hairs had begun to streak through his dark hair—put there by his kids, he'd once told Holly. But Holly doubted that—his three kids, two boys and one girl, were angelic, scrubbed-face little darlings. Holly had met them many times when they'd stopped by the dealership with their mother, Sara Beth.

Holly had hated losing him as her prime mechanic. Motor oil ran in his veins. The man was a genius with cars. But there was no sense in crying over spilled milk. Luther worked for Jack now.

She'd just be happy if he got the car running.

Holly folded up the blanket and stowed it back in the trunk of the car while the two men consulted under the hood. After what seemed like an endless amount of time and tinkering they crowed with success and slapped each other on the back.

Jack climbed into the driver's seat and started the engine. To Holly's delight it fired up and purred like a kitten. She'd get home tonight after all.

"So what was wrong with the car?" she asked. "And will it get us all the way back to town?"

If not, she was riding back with Luther. Jack could take his chances with the MG.

"It just needed Luther's magic touch," Jack said, clapping the man on the back again.

Luther gathered up his tools. He still hadn't looked Holly straight in the eye. Holly understood his embarrassment.

"Thank you for rescuing us, Luther," she said, meaning it.

That got her a quick glance from him, probably the best he could do, considering the ticklish situation he found himself in.

"He's the best damned mechanic a man could ask for," Jack said, intent on singing Luther's praises.

"Or *woman*," Holly added and went to sit in the car.

She was totally miffed at Jack—and the man would be lucky if she didn't kill him on the drive home.

Holly made her way into work Monday morning—late. She was *never* late. She didn't *like* being late. She'd never been *late* before. But Jack had inveigled his way into her life somehow—and now her life was no longer her own.

She hadn't killed him on the drive home—but she wasn't thanking him for the horrible day she'd spent in his company either. He'd driven up her bid at the auction, stranded them along the side of the road in the MG, kissed her senseless in the creek and reminded her pointedly that Luther was *his* mechanic and not hers. The worst of his crimes, however, was *the kiss*.

And she wasn't going to forgive him for it now or ever.

She slammed the door of her Thunderbird and started for the showroom door. She jerked it open, hoping her sales crew were occupied elsewhere—but no. They were all there, T.R. among them.

She pasted on a smile and sidled past them all, hoping they didn't ask her about her weekend. She didn't need her staff knowing she'd been consorting with the enemy.

Holly should fire herself as head of Hanford Motors.

She slammed into her office, went directly to the front window and clicked the blinds closed. Permanently. She did *not* want to see Jack across the street. She did *not* want to see Jack ever again. The man had taken advantage of her, stolen her mechanic, kissed her senseless and made her want to commit mayhem.

She might not be able to dislodge him from across the street, but she was determined to dislodge him from her life.

Starting today.

Now.

This very minute.

She sat down at her desk and forced herself to concentrate. First, she made arrangements for the Ghia to be picked up and delivered to the lot that week. Next, she arranged for new advertising in every major newspaper in the area. She'd find the money somewhere to cover the ads.

She couldn't let Jack get ahead of her, couldn't let her business go down the drain.

Then she started returning phone calls.

That took up what was left of her abbreviated morning.

Her mind had tried to wander—but she'd reined it in.

She still had work in her In Box, enough to keep her busy for three months, but she had a lunch date at noon with her friend Leah. And Holly intended to keep it.

She needed the diversion.

At ten till twelve she shoved the rest of her work aside. She picked up her purse, checked herself in the mirror in the small bathroom off her office to be certain Jack's kisses didn't show on her face and headed out. Through the back door, avoiding the showroom. And any possible sighting of Jack across the street.

The restaurant was crowded by the time she arrived, something Holly had expected. The place was newly opened and half the town wanted to try it out. Also, the word had gotten out that the food was terrific.

Leah found her a moment later in a quiet booth in the back. It had been months since Holly had taken time for herself, time to catch up on old friendships. Jack moving in across the street had called a halt to most everything she enjoyed lately.

"I was beginning to think you'd dropped off the face of the earth," Leah said as she hugged her, then took a seat across from her in the narrow booth.

"I know—and I'm sorry. I've just been so busy. I apologize."

It was partially the truth. Holly had been busy with work—but Jack was the reason. It required all of her attention just to keep one step ahead of the man and that left little time to think of anything else.

Then there was yesterday . . .

Forget yesterday.

"So, how have you been?" she asked Leah and then listened as her friend outlined her life, her job at the bank, her husband Mark, and their three-year-old daughter Amy.

Holly often envied her friend's happiness and her strong grasp on her dreams, all of which she seemed to have accomplished effortlessly. For as long as Holly could remember, Leah had wanted marriage and a baby.

Holly had once had those same dreams herself—but not any more. Her dreams now were about Hanford's and making her small business the success she envisioned. But now even those dreams were threatened.

Threatened by Jack.

Speaking of the devil . . .

Holly gave a silent groan as she glanced up and saw Jack striding across the restaurant—in their direction. Maybe he wouldn't see her. She considered dropping her fork and climbing under the table to retrieve it.

But Leah was already following her gaze.

"Isn't that Jack Murdock?" she asked.

Holly wanted to deny it, but Jack had spotted them and was headed toward their booth.

Did he have to choose *this* place to eat? Of course, it was the newest place in town—which was the reason Holly and Leah had chosen to come here. Still . . . she would have expected the man to have brown-bagged it, wolfing down a half-stale bologna sandwich at his desk.

Holly had no choice but to introduce him to her friend. Jack offered Leah one of his charming, sell-a-car smiles—and Leah was taken in by him, judging by the silly grin pasted on her face.

"Sorry I can't join you ladies," he said, "but I'm meeting someone."

Who was he meeting? The sexy blond bombshell from his TV commercials, Miss Headlights? Holly seemed to have forgotten her recent vow to ignore Jack Murdock.

She shouldn't care *who* he was meeting.

"Some other time, Jack," she breezed, glad that he was leaving.

Still her gaze trailed after him.

He shook hands with a man in a smart business suit before taking a seat opposite him. A business meeting, she deduced as the man produced a portfolio and the two got down to work.

But her relief that his luncheon date wasn't the blond bombshell from his tacky TV commercials quickly turned to a newfound worry. If Jack was conducting business, it somehow spelled trouble for her and Hanford's.

She remembered the phone call she'd gotten from the attorney, Mr. Eberhardt—and her fear that Jack was somehow involved.

She scrutinized the pair as if she could divine their conversation and determine if it meant trouble for her.

Why couldn't Jack have taken his annoying establishment to some other part of town? Or better yet, into the next county—where she wouldn't have to deal with him.

"That man is *gorgeous*," Leah gushed and fanned herself with her hand. "If I wasn't already married . . ."

"He's the enemy, Leah. He's turning my life upside down."

Leah's gaze returned to Jack across the restaurant. "I can see why."

Holly gave a groan. "Not like that—he's ruining my business. Haven't you seen his TV commercials?"

"Yeah—and I'd buy a car from that man any day." Then she caught what she was saying. "Sorry—if I was buying a car, of course I'd buy it from you, Holly."

She didn't say it like she meant it—and Holly sighed. Jack could tempt any woman into buying anything from him. But she could hardly blame Leah for falling under Jack's spell.

Holly had been a fool for the man herself only yesterday.

"I think you should go for him, Holly. Have a fling. You haven't dated anyone since . . . well, since . . . Adam."

"That's by choice, Leah. Adam was charming, too—and look what happened to my life. I thought he loved me, but he was only out to gain control of Hanford's."

"So, now all men mean danger?"

Holly hesitated. "I'm just not sure who I can trust—so I'm better off without a man in my life."

Leah looked at her as if she were throwing her life over a cliff. They'd been friends since they were small, their mothers friends even before that. Leah knew her only too well. But what Leah didn't understand, couldn't, was how frightened Holly was of being hurt again.

Leah had been there for her after Adam, had helped pick up the pieces of that shattered woman Holly had become then—and she loved her friend for it.

But she couldn't allow herself to fall for another man.

Especially Jack Murdock.

They finished their lunch and both of them ordered coffee. Then they talked, talked about everything but Holly's future, everything but men she should or shouldn't have a fling with.

Holly was careful not to glance across the restaurant at Jack, and if Leah noticed that, she didn't mention it. Leah might not understand her thinking—but she was her friend.

A good friend.

Chapter Seven

Jack edged the big cowboy toward one of the best truck buys on Mad Jack's lot—a dark-green Dually. Perfect for his customer's large size. The guy wouldn't even have to remove his ten-gallon hat to crawl into this baby. There was headroom galore.

The man circled the truck, looking it over with a critical eye—and Jack was hopeful. He wanted a sale. But after giving the tires an appraising kick, the guy pronounced it was "too much truck."

The morning sun beat down, hot and steamy, and Jack wanted to strip off his bright, purple-hued jacket. Not his usual taste, but it took a bit of the theatrical to sell cars. Though he had to admit, Holly sold cars without any theatrics whatsoever. Just that tantalizing allure of hers was all it took.

He gave a quick glance across the street, hoping for a glimpse of the woman who had him in such a tizzy, but there was no sight of her. She must be in her office, knee-deep in paperwork—or worse, plotting an end run around Mad Jack's.

She wasn't exactly fond of him these days, not since he'd stranded them in the MG along that secluded stretch of road, then taken advantage of the situation by kissing her senseless.

Or maybe she was miffed at herself for kissing him back.

He hadn't forgotten the taste of those kisses. The memory had kept him tossing and turning every night since. The feel of her body pressed against his. Those enticing curves he'd only just begun to explore.

He wondered just what might have happened if Luther hadn't shown up when he had.

Jack called a halt to his musings. He had a vehicle to sell to Clark—that was the cowboy's name, though he'd forgotten the last name. Not a good thing to do in business—forget a customer's name.

But Holly had him rattled. He didn't have his game face on—didn't have a face at all. Or a thought he could call his own. He'd never been so hot and bothered by a female before. And he had to get a grip.

"Uh, Clark, let me show you another set of wheels over here—a sweet little deal, if I do say so myself." Jack steered the paunchy cowboy over to a sweet-purring long-bed truck. Not as much headroom for the old ten-gallon, but Jack thought he could smell a deal.

Clark climbed inside—and as Jack had predicted—the headliner put a new crease in the cowboy's pearl-gray Stetson, something he was none-too-happy about, either.

Jack was going to have to do better if he wanted to make a sale.

Clark reworked the felt, trying to get his headgear back to its original well-formed shape, while Jack looked around the lot. He'd showed him everything of any size he had to show. "Can I interest you in an SUV?" he asked hopefully.

Clark clapped his hat back on his head and spotted the MG. "What about that little red buggy over there?" he asked, totally ignoring Jack's SUV suggestion.

"What about it?" Jack returned gruffly.

91

No matter how badly he wanted to make a sale, the MG was not it. Luther had it up and running sweetly. The little car had had just a minor carburetor glitch that day on the road, which Luther had solidly fixed. But before he could steer Clark away, the man made a beeline for the MG.

Jack groaned and trailed after him at a fast clip, catching up to him just as he reached for the door handle. He slapped his hand over the cowboy's. "You don't want this car."

"Why not? I got a girlfriend who'd just love this hot little number."

Jack cringed. First of all, he couldn't picture the aging cowboy with a girlfriend. And secondly, he didn't want the fellow using it to get in good with some woman.

"Trust me—she wouldn't like this car. It has a mind of its own. It sputters at every stop sign it meets and there's no place to put groceries. It has a trunk the size of a walnut," he lied and hoped that would be deterrent enough for the man to think about.

If not, Jack just might have to get violent.

He wasn't selling him the MG.

He wasn't selling *anyone* the MG.

It belonged to Holly.

Jack spent another thirty minutes showing the guy a few other good deals, but to no avail. He had nothing on the lot that could tickle Clark's checkbook. Not the tan SUV, the low-mileage Silverado, not even the hot little Caddie he'd just gotten in.

Then a thought came to mind. Jack glanced across the street at Holly's autos lined up neat as a pin on her lot. "Tell you what, Clark—I don't have a deal here for you, but I'm going to do you a favor. Hanford Motors has some real good buys across the street." He pulled Holly's business cards out of his jacket pocket, cards he'd filched off her desk when she wasn't looking, and handed one to Clark. "You head over there and ask for Holly. She'll fix you up with a very good set of wheels. Just be sure and tell her I sent you. You got that?"

Jack knew when he'd made a good move.

And this one was a super-duper.

He'd have Holly eating out of his hand in no time at all.

He slapped Clark on the back of his pearl-buttoned cowboy shirt and wished him well.

As Jack watched the guy head across the street, he had a warm fuzzy feeling in his dark heart.

Holly sent Clark Willets on his way a happy man.

She'd sold him a solid, heavy-duty truck and taken his old one in trade. With a little work by her repair and paint departments, it would soon be out on Hanford's lot.

What Holly couldn't believe was that Jack had sent her the customer. Was he turning over a new leaf? Did he play well with others, after all?

Or did the man have an ulterior motive?

The latter, she decided, was the most likely answer.

Sneaky was Jack's middle name.

T.R. had everything under control out on the lot, so Holly returned to her office. Jack had done her a good turn, and she at least owed him a thank you for it. She picked up the phone and punched in his number.

Jack answered on the first ring—as if he'd been just sitting there, waiting for her call. Was she playing right into the man's hands? That was a definite possibility. She knew Jack. And she knew she couldn't trust him. A leopard didn't change his spots.

And neither did Jack.

Still, she owed him.

"Jack, I just called to thank you for the referral you sent me."

93

"Ah—so did the big cowboy buy?" His voice was low, a purr in his male throat that tricked her hormones into a dangerous ricochet. She wished she didn't always have this reaction to him.

"He did," she admitted and gave him a detail or two about the sale, careful not to divulge too much to the enemy.

"That's good, Holly. Glad to be able to help out."

Holly held the phone away from her ear and gave it a wary glance. Was this the Jack Murdock she knew and did battle with? Where was that brashness, his cockiness, the wisecracks? The man was up to something.

"Why did you send the guy over? Why didn't you keep him for yourself? I don't get it, Jack. You're not a nice guy."

She heard his sharp intake of breath. "I can be a nice guy, Holly. I *am* a nice guy."

She felt a small stab of guilt at her hurtful accusation.

"Look, Holly, I didn't have anything on my lot the guy liked, so I decided to pass the ball to you. We can work together here—if you'd just put down that shotgun of yours."

"Shotgun?"

"Just a figure of speech."

Was that the way he saw her—coming at him, primed for a shootout?

Probably.

But with Jack it paid to be armed.

"Ah—I get it now. You're looking for a cut of the sale, aren't you, Jack?"

"Nope. Not at all. It's your deal, one hundred percent."

"Then what, Jack? You're after something."

"Why, Countess—you crush me. I'm just trying to return a favor."

"What favor? I've never done you a favor."

"Well, then it's time to change that."

94

Holly suspected trouble was coming. "And how am I supposed to do that, Jack?"

"Have dinner with me Saturday night."

"Dinner . . . ?" So that was what the man was up to. Send her a customer and she'd be putty in his hands. Well, she'd been putty in his hands on the trip back from the car auction. And it wasn't going to happen again if she could help it.

"Remember you owe me one, Hanford."

She should tell him to go jump in the nearest lake. He'd sent her Clark Willets. And it had been a profitable sale. But did that mean she owed him one? In Jack's book it did.

And it was a sneaky way to get a date with her.

Holly paused. She remembered her vow to avoid Jack like she would a fatal disease. But she'd walked right into this one. And being in Jack's debt was *not* the best situation to be in.

She caved. "Okay, Jack—dinner Saturday night. As long as you're on your best behavior."

"I'm always on my best behavior," he said, sounding totally affronted.

"Jack Murdock, you don't know the meaning of the word."

She hung up the phone, wondering what had happened to that lake she was going to tell him to jump into?

She'd just accepted a date with the man.

Jack purred the little red MG into Holly's driveway. A white lacy curtain parted upstairs and he caught a quick glimpse of her. She'd heard the sound of the MG.

Jack was looking forward to this date. So maybe he'd had to pull a fast one to get her to accept, but the point was, she had. Now if he could just convince her he was a nice guy. She didn't exactly think highly of him. And he had to persuade her otherwise.

That meant he'd have to be on his best behavior tonight as he'd promised. That meant not kissing that sweet mouth of hers—unless it was a chaste goodnight kiss when he brought her home.

He rapped once on the front door, and when she answered it, his breath caught in his throat. She was temptation walking in that slim-fitting dress that didn't hide one sexy curve, the color a green hue that matched the shimmer in her eyes.

She wore her hair up, fastened with a jeweled clip he intended to loosen before the night was over—if he was lucky. Then he remembered the promise he'd made about being on his best behavior. Damn, but that promise put a damper on things.

"Right on time, Jack," she said.

"Of course—being punctual is only one of my many fine attributes, Hanford. Want me to enumerate the rest of them?"

Her frown told him she didn't.

"Is the MG still in running form—or am I going to find myself stranded on another deserted road tonight?" she asked him as she grabbed up her light wrap and purse from the hall table and stepped out into the night.

"That's a tempting thought," he said. "I'll see what I can do."

She groaned as she slid into the little car, a sexy sound that had Jack's heart hammering a mad tattoo behind his ribcage. Come to think of it, that was generally its rhythm pattern whenever Holly was around.

"Where are we going tonight?" she asked.

"I thought we'd try Vincini's." The restaurant was out from town, a secluded little hideaway along the river, full of ambience and charm. And elegant—to fit the woman he was with.

The smile she wore told him she approved of his choice. Now—if he could just get her to approve of *him*.

She leaned her head back against the seat, exposing the slender column of her neck to the moonlight and the warm night air. Damn, but she was a beauty. Jack was beginning to wish he hadn't made that behavior promise.

The night slid past them as he left the outskirts of town. Ahead of him, the road curved gently and the little MG took it in stride. Ten minutes past the lights of the town, he turned into the restaurant's graveled drive. He found a spot to park near the door and helped Holly out.

They got a table in an intimate little corner—which Jack had requested when he'd made the reservation. He'd sold the maître d' a great-running little car last week and promised the guy a generous tip tonight if he could oblige him, a tip Jack surreptitiously slipped him when he seated them.

Behind Holly's back, the guy gave Jack a thumbs-up sign before leaving them alone. Jack wasn't sure if it was a signal wishing him good luck—or that he approved of the woman he was with. Probably both, Jack deduced.

"The salmon's supposed to be good here," Holly said. "I think that's what I'll have."

"Me, too," Jack replied and also ordered a good white wine to go with it.

"Have you heard any more from the attorney about the offer for Hanford's?" Jack asked. He didn't want to discuss business tonight, but he thought the offer had been strange—and he was concerned for Holly. Obviously someone wanted Hanford Motors—and badly.

"No. Nothing more." Then she narrowed her eyes at Jack. "You swear on your life it isn't you?"

It stung him that she could think that of him. "Look, I'm doing good to keep my own little enterprise afloat."

Holly studied the man across from her. He looked like he was telling the truth—but then Jack could charm a snake. She hated mistrusting people. It wasn't her usual nature. But after Adam she no longer went through life like a Pollyanna.

Still, she wanted to trust Jack.

He had on a navy double-breasted blazer that deepened the blue of his eyes—and made him seem as honest as the town banker. She was glad to know he owned something beside those ugly jackets he sported on Mad Jack's lot.

He'd undone the buttons when he sat down, and his crisp, white shirt beneath emphasized his narrow waist—which she didn't need to be admiring, she decided. Jack's good looks were dangerous enough without taking in the way his clothes fit his sexy body.

His tie was modest, no power red tonight, instead it was a seductive silver-gray, the knot perfect and not a gravy spot in sight. Maybe there was hope for the man yet.

Their waiter had returned with their wine and Holly sipped at hers. She was glad Jack had chosen this place. It was one of her favorite restaurants, but she seldom had time to dine here. Hanford's kept her too busy.

So did keeping a wary eye on Jack.

"How's the ranch coming along?" she asked to keep her mind off Jack's handsome good looks, his too-sensual body *and* his horrid establishment across from hers.

"I bought three horses the other day and a pair of saddles," he said with enthusiasm. "Do you ride?"

"Not since I was a twelve," she admitted. She'd won several ribbons in the county fair for horsemanship and jumping and she'd forgotten how much she loved to ride.

"Come out to the ranch tomorrow," he said. "We can saddle up two of the horses and make an afternoon of it."

His voice was a velvet promise she needed to ignore.

"I stay pretty busy, Jack."

Jack knew that and he wondered why. "You take life way too seriously, Holly. You need to let loose and have some fun *sometime.*"

"I don't have time for fun."

"My point exactly. I'll have the horses ready—come out and ride tomorrow. Whatever you have to do can wait, I'm sure."

She gave him a frown. "I'll give it some thought," she said, making no outright promise.

Jack let the matter drop, but he hoped she'd take him up on the invitation. He meant what he said. She was far too busy, far too often—and she could use some fresh country air to make her forget business for a while.

Their salmon was excellent. The wine, perfect. Their table, small and cozy. And Holly seemed to be enjoying herself. "Mmm—this is delicious," she said, taking a bite of her salmon. "And the fettuccine is perfect."

"I've been wanting to try this place for a long time. I'm glad you approve."

Holly smiled. "I pictured you as a guy who'd prefer a thirty-two ounce Texas steak."

"I'll have that for dessert," he said.

The restaurant lived up to its reputation. Jack enjoyed the dinner and he enjoyed Holly seated across from him, looking sexier than any woman he'd ever known. And that was a danger, he was sure. He didn't know where all this was leading him, just that he was in for the ride.

Jack ordered them each an after-dinner drink, and after a few sips of the delicious liqueur, Jack lured her to the dance floor, his hand planted at her waist.

A band played on the open patio. The night air was fresh and silky. Tiny white lights were strung in the surrounding trees, giving the dance floor an ephemeral atmosphere.

Holly felt luxurious in his arms. He held her close for the slow dance and she fit delightfully against him. "This place is perfect," he said, his voice low and throaty with want for the woman he was with.

"Perfect for what?" She leaned back and eyed him cautiously.

"Seduction, Hanford."

"In your dreams, Jack," she said with a slow smile on her face.

He twirled her out of the way of a group of dancers. "If you knew my dreams of late, sweetheart, there'd be a hot blush on that pretty face of yours."

She glanced up at him. His eyes were smiling and so was that sexy mouth of his. She remembered the feel of his kiss, teasing, tempting, and claiming. His hands drew her close, proprietary close. For the present at least she liked the feel of it, of him.

He smelled of soap and scented after-shave, a male scent that could lure a countryside of women into his lair. But with the sexy smile on his lips she knew *she* was the woman he wanted. And it was a heady feeling. If she had more sense, she'd head for cover. Jack was overwhelming her better judgment.

They moved to the music, some slow, dreamy ballad. There was no longer space between them, nor was there space for words. The music swirled in her head, her body swaying in time with it. Her eyes closed and she allowed Jack to lead her, claim her. Her left hand rested on his broad shoulder but her fingers edged upward, teasing at his thick, rich hair that curled lightly over his shirt collar.

She was lost in the music, the power of the man she was with, her senses recognizing only his closeness and this narrow world of the night that the music created.

The song ended but not the feeling of his hard body against hers. She stepped away but Jack snagged her arm. "May I have the next dance?" he asked.

Holly looked up into those compelling blue eyes of his and she was lost in their depths. She wanted another dance, too. She smiled and he took her in his arms.

He was a good dancer—but then she doubted there was anything he didn't do well. Especially when a female was involved.

Maybe it was the tiny lights in the trees and the music that created this fairyland of a place and made the evening seem so magical. He tilted her chin up and planted a kiss on her lips, a light brush, but she'd never felt anything so erotic in her life.

All too soon the music ended and the band announced a break. Holly was disappointed. It had been so long since she'd danced—and never with a man who could stir her like Jack.

He edged her through the crowd, that proprietary hand still at her waist. "Another drink?" he asked.

Holly was still distracted by his kiss, too distracted to trust another drink. "No—but thank you," she said. She reached for her purse. "I really should go before I turn in to a pumpkin. It's nearly midnight."

The place and the music and Jack's closeness had her reeling. She didn't trust herself around him. Jack paid their bill and they headed out into the night.

The moon played shadows across the parking lot and the trees swayed softly in the light breeze as he helped her into the MG. They drove out of the parking lot and Holly leaned her head back against the seat, still feeling very much under Jack's sensual spell.

It had been so long since she'd felt the magic of music, of dancing, of pressing herself close to hard, male thighs—Jack's thighs. He was so much a man that he made her head spin with near-giddiness.

"I had a good time tonight," she said.

"I did too," he answered. His voice was low and ragged with the very need she felt.

He drove with agility, his broad, capable hands on the steering wheel, the MG responding to his every touch. A woman would respond to him with the same acquiescence, she thought.

His profile was perfectly etched against the dark of the passing night, strong, male, and sensuous. He turned then, probably feeling her gaze on him, and smiled slowly.

He reached for her hand and placed it against his thigh, his own hand over it. His leg beneath the fabric of his silver-gray trousers was all hard muscle and male heat. She felt it beneath her hand and in his hand over hers as well. The intimacy made her head swim with dizziness and her pulses tripped crazily.

When they finally reached her front door he leaned in close and planted a whisper of a kiss on her upturned lips, a kiss that rocked her world.

"So, how did I do tonight, Countess?"

"Good, Jack. Very good." Her voice was a whisper and full of need.

"Good enough for you to invite me in?"

She closed her eyes, not wanting him to know how tempted she was to do just that. Invite him in and make wild, passionate love with him all night.

She swallowed hard against the desire in her throat.

And the fear.

"Don't press your luck, Jack," she said.

Her voice cracked with want, but she turned away and slipped inside.

She leaned with her back against the door, tempted, very tempted to open it again and tell Jack she wanted him to come in. His heat and male scent still surrounded her, teased at her. Would one night with Jack be too risky? Her heart tried to say no—but her mind knew otherwise.

She'd had a good time, enjoyed herself with Jack.

And if she had one iota of good sense she'd leave it at that.

Finally she heard him drive away and she pushed herself away from the barrier of the door. Her body still thrummed from the magic of him, his dangerous male scent, the vision of his charming smile.

And she knew she wouldn't get a wink of sleep tonight.

Jack sat for a long time in the swing on the sweeping porch at his ranch. He'd known sleep would be a long time coming so he'd pulled on a worn pair of jeans and come out to watch the stars in the black night sky.

What had happened tonight between Holly and him?

He'd felt her heat and saw the want and need in her eyes, the same want and need that harassed him and had his senses in a tight knot and his body aching.

She'd felt wonderful in his arms on the dance floor and he tortured himself with the memory of it. The taste of her lush mouth had bedeviled him and left him wanting for more of her.

Much more.

He hadn't forgotten that on the business front Holly still considered him the enemy. Someone or something had made her wary with fear, fear of being taken advantage of.

But damn—that someone wasn't him.

He'd made a few inroads tonight with her, but he didn't

kid himself that he'd won the war. No—Holly would take a lot more wooing before she was his.

His. That was a thought he liked.

And then what? Where did they go from there? They were rivals in business—did he really think that could translate into something more? That there could really be something real between them?

The women he'd dated were seldom ones he considered keeping around beyond a few dates, a good time for both, that was what it always came down to. What was it about Holly that was different?

What was it that had him thinking of sharing the nighttime stars with her from the porch on the ranch? Of making love with her here in his big four-poster bed that had seemed far too lonely for far too many nights lately?

He put his bare feet up on the porch railing and put the swing in motion. He searched the stars for some sign, some portent, but found neither. Only a strange loneliness deep inside his soul.

Why had he come here to Texas? Really come here? Had the Fates sent him for some sort of torture? To find the most beautiful woman he'd ever laid eyes on and then not to know what to do with her after he found her?

Not even the Fates could be that cruel.

This was the first place he'd lived that seemed like a home, something permanent. Certainly not the series of impersonal apartments he'd had in New York.

The porch swing creaked. He'd have to get an oilcan and take care of that, he thought. Then he thought again. He liked the sound. It fit, a homey sound in the quiet of the night. The sound marked progress in a man's thinking as he swung back and forth. No oilcan.

But had he come up with any answers to this thinking?

Was he falling in love with Holly?

Or was it lust—and he'd soon find himself moving on once again?

Jack wished he knew.

Chapter Eight

Holly arrived at Jack's ranch the next morning to find two horses saddled and ready to ride. Jack was standing nearby, looking tall and male gorgeous in the sunlight, the smile on his face wide and dangerous.

She climbed out of her car. "Why do you have the horses saddled? I never said I was coming," she said by way of a greeting—though she doubted he was deserving of one.

He strode over to meet her, looking entirely too mesmerizing for comfort. "It's my charm, Hanford," he said. "I knew you wouldn't be able to resist my dazzling company today."

The man was incorrigible. She should turn around and leave right now. "Jack Murdock, has anyone ever told you that you have an over-inflated ego?"

"Just you, Hanford—just you."

Holly hadn't even known she was coming this morning. She'd just found herself at loose ends, feeling strangely restless, her whole day looming ahead of her with nothing to do. She didn't want to admit her restlessness was because of Jack and their date last night. The man would love that—and she wasn't about to give his exasperating ego any more ammunition.

"Come on, Hanford, let's ride. The morning is already half gone."

She trailed after him to the corral where the horses were tethered. They were both beauties, she had to admit. One a roan and the other a pinto. The pinto tossed his head and whinnied, but the roan nuzzled at her hand, no doubt looking for a treat.

Apparently Jack thought so, too. He forced his hand into his tight jeans pocket and pulled out an apple quarter. "Feed her this and she'll be your friend for life," he said, handing the treat to Holly.

The roan took the apple from her and munched noisily. "You have table manners like your master," she told the mare and gave her a pat on her nose.

"I heard that," Jack said, giving her an aggrieved look.

"Do they have names?" she asked. "Or do I just call them horsey?"

"You're in true fighting form today, Hanford," he told her, then smiled. "This is Geronimo," he said indicating the pinto, "and this is Miss Daisy. Daisy eats her weight in food every day so she needs the exercise."

Holly laughed. "Which one did you saddle for me?"

"I'll ride Geronimo. He might be too much horse for you. Daisy's a sweetheart. Besides, it looks like you two have bonded. Ready to mount up?"

"I'm ready."

He helped her up on Daisy's back and Holly patted the horse's mane to remind her they were friends.

The trail wound itself around behind the stables and up a slight rise. They rode side by side, until the trail narrowed, necessitating single file for a distance. The scenery was lovely, with rolling plains of prairie grass, live oaks and the occasional outcropping of rock.

"I see why you bought the ranch. The land is beautiful."

"Thank you," he said. "It's good to hear that you find *something* I do right."

"Oh—you do a few things right," she said, remembering his kiss and the way he'd held her close on the dance floor.

But she quickly shook that thought from her mind. Jack was studying her intently, as if curious what she meant, but the trail narrowed again.

"Look out for the loose rock," he told her as he pulled ahead into single file again.

Holly was careful Miss Daisy didn't make a misstep but she seemed as agile as a mountain goat. The sun was warm, the air fresh and Holly was beginning to relax. Jack was right; she *did* spend far too much time working and not enough time simply enjoying herself. And she was enjoying herself, she realized.

Jack was impacting her life—but was that a good thing or a bad thing? It didn't matter, as long as she kept this just a shared day for both of them. Jack was still her rival. She'd be wise to remember that.

They were back to riding side by side. A small brook cut through the land here—and everything seemed so tranquil, so still. "Want to take a break and water the horses?" Jack asked her.

"Yes," she said and reined in Miss Daisy.

Jack dismounted and so did Holly. He took the reins of both animals and led them toward the brook. He looked like he fit the land, she thought and spent a few minutes just admiring the man in his element. He was dressed in faded jeans, nearly white from washings, and they fit him like a second skin. His shoulders were broad in his striped shirt. His muscles bunched as he let the horses drink.

Holly stepped to the edge of the water and watched, enjoying the tranquil scene. "I would think the ranch would be a full-time operation for you," she said.

He glanced over at her. "It will be someday. I want to buy some cattle when I get the fencing repaired."

"Then you won't have time for Mad Jack's." It wasn't a question but a statement. One she hoped was accurate—and soon.

"I can handle it, too," he said with a smile. "I'm an over-achiever from way back. Probably because I had to look out for my mom and sisters after my dad died."

He took a water container from a saddlebag draped over Geronimo's haunches, unscrewed the cap and handed it to her. Their hands touched and awareness flashed between them. Holly wanted to deny the response but it was there for both of them to see.

She took a swallow of the water and handed the container back to Jack. His gaze stayed fixed on hers for a long moment, then he took a drink and screwed the cap back on and tucked it into the saddlebag.

The horses were grazing on the grass so Holly sat down by the brook. Jack did, too, leaning his back against a tree. He looked at ease with himself and with life. And he probably had the right to. He'd been a genius on Wall Street, from what she'd heard, though not from Jack. He had a giant ego and could be full of himself at times, but he was surprisingly quiet when it came to his successes in life.

He'd make both the ranch and Mad Jack's work—and Holly would need to be careful. Jack was a formidable opponent.

She had her own talents, yes, but she was a near novice when it came to business. Unlike Jack. She had the feeling he turned everything that came his way into gold. He would do so with the ranch. And with Mad Jack's.

She plucked a blade of soft grass. "Your over-achievement

is making my life a nightmare," she said, and realized she'd spoken the fear aloud.

"Holly, you're losing your fighting spirit."

She shredded the grass and let it fall from her fingers. "Right," she said, then stood up, dusting off the back of her jeans. "Let's ride. Before I lose all of it."

She needed to put herself and Jack back on adversarial footing.

Where they fit much better.

The ride took them to the far back part of the ranch. Jack felt alive out here in a way he never had back in New York. The ranch held some kind of permanence for him—something else that was new to him.

And he had Holly—at least for the day.

She sat well in the saddle, tall and straight—looking strikingly beautiful in the sunlight. She wore her hair down, its strands gently tossed by the wind. Her gorgeous slender legs were sheathed in the tightest denim he'd ever seen, not that he was complaining. She wore a snap-buttoned, flower-sprigged blouse that draped softly over her breasts, the sleeves long to shade her arms from the sun.

He loved the feminine scent of her, her soft smile when she deigned to let him see it. She kept pace with him on Daisy. She rode well. It was a skill Jack had only recently mastered but Holly looked like she'd been born in the saddle.

Geronimo stopped to munch some leaves on a low-hanging tree branch, balking into a stubborn standstill despite Jack's serious nudges. "You know, you were replaced by the automobile," he said, leaning forward over the horse's mane with a loud whisper into his ear.

Behind him he heard Holly's soft laugh. He had to look ridiculous, talking to a horse that had a mind of its own. Apparently Holly thought so too, considering her laughter.

Jack turned around to give her a glower. "I could use a bit of advice here," he told her.

"No way," she said. "You're on your own, City Boy."

The horse munched away at the leaves, oblivious to both of them—or the need to move on. The day was heating up and they hadn't covered the entire ranch. Not that his ranch was all that large in acreage, but rather a long, narrow parcel bought from his closest neighbor. They shared the creek and Jack had the right-of-way to get to the back parcel that spread out somewhat. That's where they were headed now. If Geronimo finished his meal before nightfall.

"I thought you said Miss Daisy was the horse with the appetite," Holly said, trying to keep the amusement out of her voice.

"Guess, I was wrong."

"Maybe he doesn't like his feed and prefers something fresh in his diet."

He frowned over at her. "Now I have to hire a dietician for him?"

"Just trying to be helpful, Jack," she said.

After half a dozen more healthy munches, Geronimo responded to Jack's booted jabs to his flanks and the snap of the reins and moved on in a slow lope, munching the last of the tree bough he'd pulled from the tree as he went. "You are just one step away from the glue factory," Jack threatened his mount.

If the horse was worried he didn't show it.

"And you, Hanford—no more laughing. I don't want to hear this bit of juicy news turned into slander around town."

"My lips are sealed," she said.

"Your lips are pure temptation," he said, then leaned

111

across the space between them and planted a kiss on their rosy fullness.

Damn, but her mouth was sweet, inviting a man to linger and taste again and again. The horses didn't seem to mind the closeness or what their riders were indulging in. In fact, Jack fully exonerated Geronimo from his tree-munching routine as long as he stood still and let him taste Holly's sweetness one moment more.

"I thought we were seeing your ranch, Jack," she said in gentle reminder.

"Ah—yes, the ranch."

Holly laughed and gave him a shake of her head. "You are dreadful, Jack Murdock," she said, but she didn't seem all that put out with him.

The sun was well past midday when they reached the backside of Jack's land. He'd done well with his purchase, Holly had to admit. The brook ran sleepily along beside them for most of their ride, sometimes on Jack's acreage and sometimes on his neighbor's.

She loved the peacefulness of the place, the fresh air and sunlight, the soft-running brook—and being with Jack, she had to admit.

She'd even enjoyed that kiss.

"So what do you think of the place?" he asked her as they'd started back.

"It's terrific—and I think you should concentrate on the land and forget about selling cars," she told him.

"Not on your life," he said, giving her his best charm-a-woman smile. "I've got this little thing going with my competition across the street, which I fully enjoy."

Holly frowned. "Even if you're causing headaches for this competition of yours?"

"She's just overly-sensitive," was his answer. "She doesn't understand that I'm the best thing that could happen to her."

"You're a pain in the neck, Jack. And you sure know how to ruin a perfectly good day." She gave Miss Daisy a snap of the reins and sent her into a gallop, leaving Jack behind to eat her dust.

It didn't take long for him to catch up. "Do I really cause you headaches?"

"Yes, Jack—on a continuing basis."

He chuckled low and deep, and it rippled over her like warm silken sand. She needed to quit reacting to the man on such a sensual level. On any level. She tried to call up her anger at him but the best she could come up with was annoyance. But even the annoyance he engendered in her had a way of slipping away when she needed it the most—like now.

Damn the man, anyway! She wished he'd take all that dangerous charm of his and disappear into the ether. But Holly couldn't be that lucky.

They had to go single file again so Jack pulled a short distance ahead of her. Holly followed along behind, trying to focus on anything other than Jack. Why had she *really* come here today? It was attraction that drew her, attraction to a man who could make her crazy, whose kisses teased at everything feminine in her.

The sun had sent the temperature soaring and she was glad they were headed back. A large glass of iced tea beckoned to her and a spot of cool shade. Holly wondered how much farther they had to ride. Not far, if her sense of direction was accurate. The ranch house and stables should be—

Geronimo whinnied in a banshee scream of panic and reared on hind legs. Her breath caught as Jack fought to stay in the saddle. What had frightened him? Then Holly saw the sidewinder slithering from the path. She fought to steady her own horse, frightened by Geronimo's tumult.

The horse reared again—and Jack wasn't able to hold on. He was tossed to the ground and wild scrub. But that wasn't the worst of it. Geronimo's rearing front hooves were threatening to come down on Jack's head. Holly got out a shriek. "Jack, watch out!"

Jack saw the threat and was able to roll to safety.

She jumped down from Miss Daisy and raced over to him. "Are you hurt?" Her hands went to him, feeling for damage, broken bones, his last breath of life.

"Darlin', I like what your hands are doing," he said, his voice a low male purr.

"I should let you die right here, Jack Murdock," she said, resisting the urge to inflict more injury on him than what his fall had caused.

He pulled to a sitting position, then dropped his head to his knees.

"Are you all right?" she asked. Maybe he *was* hurt and she felt a stab of remorse for her threat.

"Just a little woozy. Give me a minute. I'll be okay."

But he didn't look like he'd be okay. He had paled. Cuts and scratches covered his arms, his hands. He had a gash on his right cheek that had begun to bleed. "Jack, you're hurt!"

Her hand went to his cheek and he winced.

He dragged a handkerchief from a pocket but couldn't quite get it to the wound. "Here, let me," she said and pressed it to his cheek to stanch the bleeding. "We need to get you back to the ranch. Can you ride?" she asked.

"Of course I can ride—as soon as I kill that damned sidewinder."

Holly gave a smile. "Too late—he took off for the brook."

"Smart move." He looked around for Geronimo. Apparently the horse had recovered faster than Jack. He stood a short distance away, nibbling leaves from yet another low-lying tree branch, reins dragging in the dirt.

He strode over to his horse, snapped up the reins and climbed aboard.

"Are you sure you can ride? I don't want to see you take another tumble," Holly said, keeping a close eye on Jack who still had her worried. "You might not survive the next time."

The man was so damned macho he wouldn't admit to a weakness of any sort. She retrieved Miss Daisy's reins and mounted up. She hoped the ranch house was nearby.

It wasn't far, and when the stables came into view, she gave a sigh of relief. Jack had to be hurting from his fall. He insisted on pulling the saddles from the horses, though Holly could have done that. "Come on, I need to get you into the house and clean up those scrapes of yours," she said.

"You going to put your sweet hands all over me again?"

Holly frowned. "No—just around your neck, Jack."

He gave a low laugh but allowed Holly to drag him toward the ranch house. She was concerned about him; she couldn't hide that behind her stinging retorts, and Jack was definitely pleased that she was. Now if he could just turn that concern into something more—like wanting his sexy body. If Holly knew his thoughts at the moment she'd rail at him about them.

"Into the bathroom, Jack. Let's get those cuts and scratches cleaned up," she ordered. "Do you have a first-aid kit?"

"In the bathroom," he answered.

He dragged off his dirty shirt and tossed it in the hamper. A glance in the mirror over the sink showed the nasty gash on his right cheek from landing in the scrub. His arms and hands sported bloody scratches covered with dirt and bits of rock. But only the gash on his cheek looked like it was of any consequence. "Think this will mar my handsome good looks, Hanford?" he asked.

"It won't put a dent in them. Now wash—or I'll do the job for you."

"Promises, promises," he said and took up a wash cloth to lightly scrub away the trail dirt and dust from his face and arms. He felt the sting from the soap, but he was tough; he could take it.

Holly picked up a blue towel and dabbed the areas dry. "I'm a little concerned about your cheek. It looks like it could use a few stitches."

He raised his hands in defense. "Not on your life, sweetheart—no stitches."

She gave him an arched smile. "What's the matter, Jack? Afraid of a little needle?"

"No—just doctors in starched white coats."

"Wuss," she teased.

She finished drying his arms, then dabbed his wounds with peroxide. It bubbled and stung—but he wouldn't give Holly the satisfaction of knowing that. After all, he was tough. No wuss. Not at all.

Besides, did he want to give up the opportunity of having her so close, her sweet hands touching him? Not on his life. If he knew he'd get this much attention from her, he'd have tumbled off Geronimo's back a few more times.

She uncapped the small tube of antibiotic ointment from the first-aid kit and spread each wound with the medication, but all Jack noticed was the soft touch of her fingers as they brushed over his scrapes and scratches. Just the feel of her touch would heal them, he was sure. Jack had it bad when just a whisper of her fingertips on him could evoke all kinds of fantasies in his head. She dressed his injuries with gauze and tape. But even through the gauze he could feel her sensual touch.

That done, she turned her attention to his right cheek.

"I'd really feel better if you'd get stitches in this one," she said.

Jack wanted to feel her hands on him again. Not some doc in the emergency room with hands far less intriguing than Holly's. "Just patch me up," he said.

The man was stubborn. At least his color was better, Holly decided. The paleness that had worried her earlier had left him. She'd do the best she could with his cheek and hope it would heal without a scar.

Touching Jack, feeling his warm skin beneath her fingertips, had left her more than a little shaky. Maybe breathless was a better word. Hot, even more apropos. His tanned skin was dangerous, with very male muscles beneath.

"All right," she said reluctantly. "If you say so. Do you want a bullet to bite on?"

"Sweetheart, if I gave you a bullet you'd find a way to fire it into me."

She gave him a small smile. "Don't give me any ideas, Jack." She returned her attention to her patient, trying to keep her mind on what she was doing, but with her hands all over the man, it was difficult.

She pulled out a few butterfly bandages from the first-aid kit. "I think I'll use these and pull the edges together to approximate stitches, since you won't go get them."

"Just do it," he argued.

She touched his cheek in a gentle pull, bringing the edges of the cut together. His skin was warm and he smelled of the soap he'd just washed with. She could feel his breath on her hands. His tanned bared chest made her struggle for composure. She didn't need Jack knowing he could affect her the way he did.

117

A moment later she had finished and stepped back to admire her handiwork. "Do you have scrapes anywhere else?" she asked, eyeing his dusty torn jeans.

Jack followed her line of vision to his jeans, jeans he didn't want to shuck in front of her. "No way, sweetheart. I'm not stripping out of these unless it's for a trip between the sheets, not for you to put a bandage on a scratch."

"Fine," she said. "Get gangrene—see if I care."

She tucked the items back in the medical kit and set it aside, then started out of the bathroom. Jack called out to her retreating backside. "There's some fresh lemonade in the refrigerator. Pour yourself a glass while I go find some clean clothes."

Holly had patched the man up to the best of her abilities. Now she should leave, but a cool glass of lemonade did sound good. It took her a few wrong turns but she found the kitchen at the back of the house. Next to it was the dining room, empty of furniture at the moment, but she could picture a room filled with chairs and table large enough to hold family gatherings.

The kitchen was a good size too, with lots of cabinets and an eat-in breakfast nook tucked against a back wall. The style was rustic, but homey. Very homey. She opened the refrigerator and found the pitcher of lemonade, but very little else. Apparently Jack didn't spend much time honing his culinary skills. Not that that surprised her much. She pulled out the pitcher, found glasses in the cabinet, none of which matched. Neither did the few dishes in the next cabinet. He had a few pots and pans, all battered and old.

Jack Murdock could use a woman in his life, she thought. Not that she was volunteering for the job. *No way!* The man was impossible and irked her to no end.

She grabbed ice cube trays in the freezer and emptied a

few cubes into the glasses then poured the lemonade. Holly took a long swallow of hers. It felt good sliding down her parched, dusty throat. She topped off her glass with more, then placed the pitcher back in the near-empty refrigerator and went to investigate the remainder of the house.

The living room was wide and spacious, with warm paneling and high beamed ceilings. The furnishings were a hodge-podge of styles, but comfortable looking. A big leather couch one could sink into and two comfy chairs.

A large stone fireplace dominated the room and Holly could imagine her and Jack snuggled before it on a cool evening. What was she thinking? Whatever it was, it was a dangerous thought. One she needed to put out of her mind—and fast.

A few framed pictures rested on the fireplace mantel. Curious about them, Holly took a peek at them. Maybe they'd give her a clue as to who the man really was—down deep. She saw a photo of Jack with two women. His sisters? A good guess, she decided when she saw them in several other pictures surrounded by kids and husbands. There was a photo of an older woman—his mother, no doubt, and beside it an older picture of a man she was certain must be his father. The man looked very much like Jack, with broad shoulders and the same roguish smile his son had. She remembered Jack telling her his father had died when Jack was young. She suspected it was a photo he cherished.

She stepped away from the mantel and hugged her arms to herself. Spending the day with Jack, kissing him on the trail, feeling his warm, bare skin beneath her fingertips as she patched him up just now, was all too much for her.

She took another sip of her lemonade. Her thirst quenched, along with her curiosity, she should leave, put some distance between Jack and the way he made her feel.

119

Before she could do anything Jack emerged from the direction of the bathroom—and his bedroom. He had clean clothes on again, a pair of black jeans that looked fresh-washed and . . . *snug.* And a blue shirt he was slowly trying to button. She wished he'd get the job done and fast. The sight of that broad chest and rippling muscles beneath were more than her senses could take. She took a long swallow of her drink, but it didn't douse her alert hormones.

"I'll grab a lemonade and we can sit on the porch and cool down from our ride," he said.

Holly needed to cool down—or better yet, leave. But before she could say anything Jack was back with the lemonade she'd poured for him. "I really should go," she said, following him out to the big, wraparound porch.

"No—stay. I'll put a pair of steaks on the grill for dinner."

Dinner was a long way off and Holly didn't trust herself to stick around in Jack's company that long. She shook her head. "Thanks, but no thanks. I have to get *some* work done before this weekend is over."

"There you go with that work again. Sit back and relax."

"I've relaxed all day," she said. "Now it's time to get ready for Monday."

"You enjoyed our ride?"

She nodded. "Thank you for inviting me." She finished the last of her lemonade and set the glass on a small wicker porch table. "And for the lemonade."

She headed for the steps before she could change her mind and take Jack up on the offer of dinner and whatever came with it. Besides she was dusty from the ride and she needed a long hot shower to relieve the ache in muscles she hadn't used for a while.

Jack caught up with her and walked her to the car. "I enjoyed today too," he said, his voice low and husky and entirely too dangerous to her senses.

She slid in behind the wheel and reached for the door to pull it closed, but Jack leaned into the car and gave her a kiss, a hot, sultry kiss that shook her equilibrium.

Time to go, she knew, past time. Way past time. Before she was tempted to stay, she gathered her resolve, put the car into gear and drove away. Jack Murdock was far too captivating for a woman to resist.

Chapter Nine

Holly made her way into her office the next morning, happy that neither T.R. nor her other salesmen were around. They were all occupied in various activities and she sincerely hoped they stayed that way for most of the day.

She hadn't been able to get Jack off her mind or out of her senses—and she didn't want her preoccupation to make anyone curious as to why she wasn't her usual self.

Jack could charm the stockings off any woman he met, she was certain. Holly had thought she could resist him—but even she'd fallen victim to the man.

She set her briefcase on her desk and opened the blinds at her front office window, then out of habit gave a quick glance across the street. Maybe seeing Jack dressed in one of his ugly jackets would break this spell she was under.

He had several customers on his lot already this morning, she noticed. Those annoying commercials of his were apparently still dragging in the gullible.

Then she saw Jack. No garishly loud jacket today. Instead he looked sexy and lean in a light-tan, well-tailored one, emphasizing his wide, sensual shoulders. She recalled the feel of those shoulders when she'd patched him up yesterday—all male, all muscle, all Jack.

He was showing a car to a woman, who was no doubt

drooling over him. And how could Holly blame her when she'd done the very same thing herself? He looked good. The breeze had ruffled his thick, dark hair. Beneath his jacket he had on a blue shirt with no tie—the shirt, she was sure, electrifying the blue of his eyes.

What had happened to his closet full of ugly jackets?

Holly snapped the blinds closed and returned to her desk, dragging the paperwork from her briefcase, paperwork she hadn't even glanced at over the weekend. Because of Jack. He had sidetracked her, rocked her mind and her senses. She pressed her fingers to her forehead where guilt over her lack of weekend work had a headache beginning to form.

So much for starting off a new week, she thought.

But Holly only had herself to blame. She knew getting involved with Jack would bring trouble. The man had slipped in under her radar screen, charming her out of her wariness; he'd gotten past the barriers she thought she had solidly in place.

At least she hadn't made love with him, not that the temptation hadn't been there. It had. But that was little consolation to her this morning. Jack affected her, a fact that was getting harder and harder for her to deny.

She spread out her work in front of her and forced herself to concentrate on it. Hanford's was doing well—despite Jack's horrid little enterprise across the street. The figures she pored over proved that.

Now, if she could only continue to make that happen.

In fact, she hoped she could improve on what the figures showed. It was nearly summer, and summer meant cars, road trips and evening drives. Her business always improved then—and she needed to capitalize on it.

It was late morning when T.R. popped his head in her office door.

"Holly—got a minute?" he asked.

"Of course, T.R." She put aside her work and offered him a smile.

He didn't return the gesture. Instead his face bore a dour expression, and Holly became worried. Was he about to resign his job with Hanford's, lured away by Jack—as Luther had been? Or planning to retire altogether like Brewer. It might be selfish on Holly's part but she *needed* T.R. and his selling expertise. She also needed his friendship and loyalty, which T.R. had always offered in spades. It had hurt to lose Luther. She didn't want to lose her chief salesman and good friend as well.

Her forehead pleated and worry skidded down her spine. "What's wrong, T.R.?"

T.R. hesitated for a long moment, frightening Holly even more. "I struggled all morning about how to tell you this," he said.

Holly drew in a sharp breath, her worry-level skyrocketing. "Just tell me," she said, trying to affect a calm she definitely didn't feel.

"It's about Hanford Motors," he said. "There's . . . a rumor going around that you've been setting back the odometers on some of your vehicles."

"What!" Holly's voice was a screech of disbelief. "But that's not true, T.R. We don't do that—and we never would. We sell good, quality used cars; it's what our reputation is based on."

"I know, I know," he said. "I've been trying to track down the source of the rumor—but so far, I haven't had any luck."

Well, Holly knew the source. Or at least she strongly *suspected* it.

Jack Murdock.

The man she'd spent most of her weekend with, dancing

with him under the stars, riding with him on his ranch, patching up his wounds after Geronimo had thrown him, *kissing* him. How could she have been such a fool? The way she'd been with Adam. Hadn't she learned her lesson the first time?

"How many people know about this, T.R.?" Holly's brain went into solution mode—if there *was* a solution.

"I really don't know, Holly," he said. "But I'm afraid it'll be all over town very soon. You know how things are around here. Rumors spread like wildfire, especially ugly rumors."

Her headache, mild until now, began to throb with a vengeance, and her usually stiff spine slumped in defeat. How could she fight a rumor like this?

And how much harm would it do?

It was a blot on her reputation, a reputation Hanford's had had ever since her father began the business years ago. They were a small dealer, but an honest one—and the town knew that. It was why she'd been so successful—at least up until now.

Would people believe the rumors?

If they did, she was afraid it would be the death knell for her and for Hanford's.

"Is there anything you want me to do?" her stalwart head salesman asked, if possible looking even bleaker than he had when he entered her office.

Holly had no idea what they *could* do. "I don't know, T.R.," she said. "Except do as much damage control as we can for now. In the meantime, I'm going to find out who started this ugly rumor."

She waited until T.R. had left her office, then with mind racing and her thoughts on a single culprit, she headed across the street to Mad Jack's.

Could he be the menace behind this? Holly hoped he

wasn't, but she had to admit, he was the person who'd benefit the most if Hanford Motors went down to ignoble defeat.

And he was just low enough to think of such a ploy.

Jack had enjoyed a successful morning. He'd sold two autos—and both for a good price, too. A great way to start out his week, he thought as he headed into the small trailer he used for an office.

His commercials were beginning to pay off, he was making a little money, and if this past weekend was any indication, Holly was warming to him. He propped his booted feet on a corner of his battered desk and leaned back in his chair.

He was just beginning to savor his accomplishments when he looked up and saw Holly storming through his office door. She had on a slim, sarong-styled dress and sexy high-heeled sandals. Her hair fell to her shoulders in a cascade of dark, glorious silk. He'd love to delve his fingers into it and plant a kiss on those ruby-red lips of hers the way he had this past weekend—but if he read the fury in her green eyes right she was in no mood for that.

What had set off her fireworks?

This time?

He couldn't think of anything *he'd* done—except for stealing those tangy little kisses from her, kisses he'd enjoyed, maybe more than he should have. "What brings you over to this neck of the woods?" he asked. "Are you here to buy the red MG?"

"Don't play games with me, Jack. You know very well why I'm here."

"No—I don't know. Why don't you tell me?" He removed his feet from the papers on his desk and sat upright. Whatever was coming his way, he needed to be ready for it.

Holly was on the attack.

And Jack was in the line of fire.

Again.

She paced around to the front of the desk and pressed her pretty hands to its surface, determined to look him straight in the eye. "Has anyone ever told you that you're one horrible, lowdown slug of a human being, Jack Murdock?"

Man! Was she mad? He placed his feet on the corner of his desk again and leaned back in his chair. "As a matter of fact, I think that was one of *your* descriptions of me the day I moved in here—along with a few other references to my nefarious character."

She gave him a dark glower. "Don't try to sidetrack me."

"Honey, I wouldn't dream of it."

That only seemed to make her madder, and if all that fury of hers wasn't being directed at him, he'd lean back and just enjoy her fire. But she had something on her mind and there wouldn't be any peace around here until she'd had her say.

"Why don't you calm down some and tell me what's got you so riled up?"

"I'll be happy to tell you, Jack. It's that despicable rumor you've been spreading about me, that I've been setting back the odometers on my vehicles."

"Have you been setting back the odometers on your vehicles?"

She planted her hands on those delightful hips of hers. "Of course, I haven't—and how dare you say that I have, you . . . you . . . *louse?*"

Now he was a louse. One step better than a slug, he decided. But he didn't kid himself that Holly was cooling off any.

She wasn't.

"Well, darlin', I hate to tell you this, but I'm not the one spreading those rumors. I've just been here, minding my own business. Not that you're going to believe that, I'm sure."

She was too mad—and too willing to think the worst of him.

"Of course, you'd lie. Why did I think you'd admit to it?" She squared her shoulders in a huff, her spine starched with rancor.

"Maybe because I'm not guilty?" he offered.

That earned him another dark glower. It stung that she thought he could be so base, so deceitful, as to try to hurt her or her company. That wasn't the way Jack played the game. He moved his feet off the corner of his desk and stood up. He wanted to go to her, pull her into his arms and tell her he'd make everything all right.

But if it was true that someone was out to do damage by spreading false rumors, he wasn't sure he *could* make things right. No matter how much he might want to.

"Look, Holly—forget for a moment that you think I did this and tell me who else might be out to cause trouble for you."

Her prim mouth opened in a sigh. For a moment she looked like she might cry—but he doubted Holly Hanford ever let loose with a flood of tears. "You're at the top of a list of one, Jack Murdock. You're the one who stands to gain from my disgrace." The last was spoken in a hushed voice, as if all that fury of hers had finally met with defeat.

And his heart broke for her. Her pride was at stake here—and he knew that loss of pride would hurt her far more than the loss of a few car sales.

"I'm not out to ruin Hanford's, Holly. I didn't do this, and whoever did is one despicable bastard. I'll check around, see what I can find out about the rumor, who might have started it and who has something to gain from it."

She turned on her heel and walked toward the door. "I

fight my own battles, Jack. Thanks, but no thanks." She offered him one last glower before she slammed out of his office.

The woman wouldn't take a drink if she was dying of thirst in the desert, Jack thought. He admired her starch and determination—but it didn't hurt to accept help once in a while. Something Holly needed to learn. The woman was stubborn to a fault, but whether she liked it or not, Jack intended to see what he could uncover on his own. He wasn't going to let Hanford's go down to defeat without a try. He liked having Holly across the street too much to let that happen.

Holly slammed back into her office and fought down the tears that threatened to spill forth. Had she made a fool of herself accusing Jack of this deceit? She didn't want to believe that the man could do something so ruthless, so vile—but neither could she allow herself to trust him.

He, alone, stood to gain from her misery.

Adam had played her for a fool once—and she couldn't allow Jack Murdock, and his wily ways, to play her for one as well. She'd promised herself she'd never let a man do that to her again.

She'd succumbed to Jack's kisses, his touch, tried to forget late at night when the memory of those kisses kept her from sleeping. But she couldn't forget the feel of him holding her against him on the dance floor, the desire that had arrowed through her when he'd kissed her at the ranch.

Was that just this weekend?

It felt like it was a lifetime ago now.

Jack was her competition, her rival—and she couldn't allow him to be any more than that. She couldn't allow herself to feel anything for him—other than fury.

And suspicion.

She felt better having resolved that in her mind. Now she needed to decide how best to deal with these rumors about her and her business. That was the hard part, the part she didn't know how to handle.

She'd taken over her father's company, and she knew how to sell cars, but how did she go about fighting injustice, damage to what she held dearest—her good name?

She hoped the rumors would die away. With nothing to fuel them but lies, maybe they would.

But Holly wasn't holding out much hope of that.

Lies had a way of sounding like truth to some. At the very least they caused doubt and distrust—and that, she knew, would not earn her any customers.

Jack had spent the past week trying to get Holly out of his mind. He'd worked the ranch until exhaustion had claimed him—and still he remembered the feel of her, the taste of her, her sultry, feminine scent. At Mad Jack's he'd stayed busy, barely allowing himself a glance across the street for fear the delectable sight of her would rattle him and cause him to lose an important sale.

He wondered if she thought of him, of the time they'd spent together, the kisses they'd shared. Or did she still think of him as the enemy? The one who'd started the rumors? The one out to undermine her business? He was sure it was the latter—despite the fact that Jack was innocent.

She hadn't wanted his help, had thrown it back in his face—not that Jack had adhered to her demand. He'd sleuthed anyway, had tried to find out who might have started the rumor, who might be out to cause her harm.

But he hadn't been able to uncover a thing.

Holly was well liked in this town. None of the other dealers he'd talked to wished her anything but continued success. Certainly he'd found no one who would spread untruths about her.

Jack slammed his desk drawer shut. It was time to close up for the night. No one would be out shopping for a good deal on a car or truck this late. But worry about Holly had kept him here way past closing time. He'd wanted to help, had hoped to find the person behind the rumor haunting her and her business. He still wanted to. But at the moment he was completely out of sources. No one was talking.

Maybe he'd stumble onto something soon, but for now, tonight, he had to admit defeat.

He climbed into the small MG and headed out of the lot. Lights were on in Holly's office, he noticed. She often stayed late, but not this late. What kept her here tonight?

Curiosity got the best of him and he pulled up in front of her showroom. She worked too hard—he'd told her that before. But Holly just gave him one of her mind-your-own-business glowers.

He slammed the door of the MG and headed into the showroom. The classiness of the place never failed to affect him. And her new addition, the cream-colored Karmann Ghia she'd bought when they'd gone to the car auction in Houston, now sat polished and spit-shined amid her other prized autos.

He sauntered over to it and gave it a quick appraisal. It was a real, little beauty—but then, had he expected anything less of Holly?

Everything she did was done well. He opened the door and slid into the seat, planting his big hands on the steering wheel.

"Are you here to buy?"

Jack heard the soft, feminine lilt that went with those

words and he slid out from the car and closed the door. "Nope—'fraid not. But she cleaned up nice," he said.

A slight smile tilted at her gorgeous lips, not at him, Jack was sure, but at what she'd accomplished with the little car. How did she do it? Everything she touched had her own personal stamp of perfection on it.

"Too bad," she said. "I'd hoped to make one more sale tonight."

Jack followed her back into her office. "You work too hard, Hanford. The world won't come to a grinding halt, if you eased up a bit."

She gave him a look that said she didn't agree. She went around behind her desk and began tossing pens and other paraphernalia into the center drawer. She stacked her work neatly—to have it ready for tomorrow, he was certain.

And she'd be here bright and early, he had no doubt.

Ready to go at it once again.

"Is this what you had for dinner tonight?" he asked, picking up a half-eaten package of vending machine crackers from the corner of her desk.

She snatched them out of his hand as if she were afraid he'd contaminate them. "I didn't have time to eat," she said.

"That's what I figured. Come on, I'm taking you out for a bite. And no excuses," he added when she opened her pretty mouth to offer an objection.

She locked her desk drawer, picked up her purse and began turning off lights. That done she gave a long sigh. "I really don't have time for dinner, Jack."

"Of course you do—everyone needs to eat. And crackers from a machine is not a substantial meal," he insisted, then ushered her out into the dark night. "Besides, if you're going to keep up your offensive with Mad Jack's, you need nourishment."

He knew that would win her over.

And it worked.

With a defeated sigh, she climbed into the MG. He hid a smug smile and closed the door he'd been holding open for her.

"What kind of a price did you put on the Karmann Ghia?" he asked as he pulled out into traffic. He was making conversation, partly because he was curious, and partly because concentrating on the Ghia was a whole lot safer than concentrating on Holly's sexy appeal.

"Do I smell a possible sale, Jack?" Her smile was wry, and he liked her that way, ready to give him a run for his money.

"If I said yes, you'd just up the price."

"Of course."

Holly felt herself relax—she and Jack were back on rival footing. And that was safer. Far safer than letting him twist and turn her hormones in the wind.

She remembered the old saying—keep your friends close and your enemies even closer. Not that she relished the idea of keeping Jack any closer than he already was.

The man was a danger to her senses.

He looked his usual sexy self tonight in a dark green polo shirt that hugged his handsome torso and accentuated his broad shoulders. His light-colored chinos hugged his muscled thighs—not that Holly should be noticing.

Strands of his dark hair ruffled in the created breeze of the little MG. His hands were broad and firm on the wheel. He was taking on a bronzed tan, probably from his work on the ranch. She suspected ranch work was the reason for his solid muscles, as well.

Her casual perusal of him was fortunately interrupted when he pulled into the parking lot of her favorite Chinese restaurant, Kim Loo's. This late at night the crowd had thinned out. They had their choice of booths and Jack picked one tucked away in a softly lit corner. Holly would have preferred a less intimate setting but she didn't want to admit she considered Jack a threat of any kind.

She knew the man's ego.

As Holly looked over the menu, she realized just how hungry she was. Snack crackers would not have appeased her appetite. They both ordered the won ton soup and almond chicken with snow peas and fried rice, then Holly leaned back in the teakwood booth.

"I've been doing some checking around to see just who might have started the rumor," Jack said, "but so far I haven't been able to find out anything."

Holly leaned forward, anger in her hot green eyes. "I told you I fight my own battles, Jack Murdock. I'll thank you to mind your own business and leave mine alone."

"Look, Holly, you don't have to fight this thing alone. I'd like to help."

"I don't need your help, Jack."

She needed someone's help—but she would never admit it.

"Have you come up with anything on your own?"

She picked up her napkin and shook it out, then placed it daintily on her lap, though their food had not yet arrived. Jack waited for her answer.

"No, nothing," she said finally. Her voice was a challenge, daring him to say a word about her lack of success after refusing *his* good, solid offer.

"Any suspicions?"

She gave him a hard look. "Besides, you—no," she said.

"Holly, I told you I didn't spread any rumor, of any kind, for any reason."

She gave what he thought was a slight nod of her head. Did

that mean she believed him? Jack doubted it—though she might be giving him the benefit of the doubt. At least for now. Probably the best he could hope for, considering Holly's low opinion of him.

Their food arrived and their conversation took on a less adversarial tone. They discussed the won ton soup, the weather and the roadwork that had snarled traffic in McCallum. She asked him about the ranch, which Jack loved to talk about, and he even had her laughing that the big city guy had gotten himself tangled up in the fence wire he was putting up—and had the wounds to prove it. Along with those from his tumble from his horse.

At least that was one city-slicker accident he hadn't repeated.

Yet.

Her laughter was soft, melodic, and it lit her eyes as well, softening them and crinkling them at the corners. She looked incredible at the end of her long day, though he knew she had to be tired. Her hair glistened in the soft light of the restaurant. Her eyes were bright and alert with only the slightest hint of dark smudges beneath them, attesting to her long hours at work.

Her slim dress was still crisp and its sleeveless style showed off her slender arms. Her legs were beneath the table now, but he hadn't missed noticing them earlier, long and sleek below the hem of her summery, silk dress. Holly was one classy lady—and he reveled in the fact that she was here with him.

"Aren't you going to open your fortune cookie?" he asked after the waiter had cleared their table and delivered the treats to them on small silver plates.

She picked up her cookie, cracked it open and pulled out the streamer inside.

"So—what does it say?" he asked when she didn't read it aloud.

She hesitated—and he saw the slightest tremor in her hand. Finally she glanced over at him. "It says, 'Trust In A Friend.' "

"You should heed the advice, Holly. I'd like to be that friend."

Holly wanted to believe him. She'd like to be able to trust in someone again, have someone to lean on—just a little.

Jack was easy to talk to—when he wasn't challenging her, sale for sale, in their respective businesses. In fact, she was enjoying tonight, her dinner with him, their easy banter.

But how far could she trust him?

He made her uneasy, worried. Not only for her business, but for her heart, as well. He could trample it—if she let down her guard. His eyes were as blue as the morning sky and looked twice as honest. But what was beneath that façade? Fake charm?

Or something real?

"I've run Hanford's myself for two years. I don't know who's spreading this ugly rumor. I don't know why that attorney called me, thinking I'd accept an offer to sell my business, but Hanford's is part of me. I grew up in that place, went to work with my dad every chance I got. I had car grease on the tip of my nose and the ends of my pigtails. If I fail, I'll fail on my own," she told him.

Jack tried to imagine Holly's nose decorated with car grease, her hair in pigtails—and the image endeared her to him all the more. Hanford's was hers and she fought like a mother bear to protect it.

He couldn't fault her for that.

But everyone needed a shoulder to lean on once in a while. And Jack was offering that shoulder. "I have a feeling this mistrust issue of yours goes far deeper than just fear of losing Hanford's, though that's bad enough," he said.

She glanced up at him, her green eyes raking over his face. "Maybe," she answered finally.

"Want to talk about it?"

Did she? Holly didn't know. It was a burden she'd carried around with her for a long time. Only a few people knew about Adam's betrayal, how he'd stolen from her father, though that was something she still couldn't prove; of how he'd tried to take over Hanford's and undermine Holly's every move.

But no one knew the personal pain she'd suffered. Nor would they. That part Holly kept tightly locked away. But she could tell Jack part of it, try to explain, hope he'd understand. And maybe, *back off*.

She topped off her cup from the small pitcher of green tea the waiter had left and took a small sip. "My father had a man who worked for him. He stayed on and tried to help me out with Hanford's. I trusted him—only to find out I shouldn't have. Adam had his own interests at heart—not mine, not Hanford's."

"What happened to him?" he asked.

"I fired him." That was easier to say than the truth, that she'd had to remove him from her personal life as well. He'd broken her heart—and damaged her trust.

But Jack didn't need to know that.

"Where is the guy now? Could he be behind any of what's going on with Hanford's?"

Holly set down her tea and gazed over at Jack, considering what he was saying, then shook her head. "No, I'm sure he's not. He left town long ago. I haven't heard from him since."

"Still—it's something to consider," Jack said.

"I don't even know where he is right now. Nor do I want to. That's in the past."

"Except that he's left you with a load of mistrust to carry on those otherwise confident shoulders of yours."

Jack did understand—maybe more than she wanted him to. His voice was low and soft and suddenly Holly wanted to feel his strong arms around her, wanted to lean on him just for a moment.

This talk of Adam had ripped the bandage off the old wound and left her feeling unsettled. She gathered up her purse. "It's late," she said. "Maybe we should go."

Jack followed Holly out of the restaurant. He'd learned a little more about what made this woman tick, but he felt there was more to her story about Adam. The man had hurt her— and not just in a business kind of way. But he was sure Holly didn't want to talk about it.

The Texas night was still warm as they made their way out into the parking lot. The stars that Jack had always heard shined bigger and brighter in this state were doing just that. They glinted off Holly's dark hair, giving it a stunning luster. Her eyes were wide—and the hurt he'd seen in them when she'd talked about Adam had dissipated some.

"You haven't opened your fortune cookie," she teased as they reached the MG.

"You're right—okay, here goes." He cracked open the cookie. "Kiss the one you're with," he read, then gave her a brash smile.

"Jack Murdock, I don't believe you for a second. I want to see your fortune." She reached for the tiny strip of paper, but Jack held it high above her, out of her reach.

"I want my kiss," he demanded.

Before Holly could object, he drew her close and wrapped

his big arms around her small frame. His mouth found hers in a light kiss, a gentle buss of her lips—but he couldn't leave it at that. Holly drove him wild with want, and he kissed her again, this time with desire he could barely rein in.

She felt so damn good against him. He'd wanted her from that first moment he saw her, ranting at him about his ugly cars and even uglier lot across the street from hers.

He'd known then that she was a woman with more passion than she knew what to do with; knew, too, that he couldn't wait to taste that passion.

Holly knew she should pull away. This was Jack. A man who'd lie about a fortune cookie was not a man she should trust. And Jack had lied, she was sure of it—lied to get her in his arms and kiss her senseless.

Again.

She shouldn't fall for his wily tricks, but she felt herself melting against that big, sturdy frame of his—couldn't stop herself from kissing him back. Her breasts tingled as he pulled her closer to him. His mouth tantalized hers, tormented her in a way she was beginning to like a little too much.

The man was a threat to her fired-up senses and she was playing right into those mesmerizing hands of his. She made a weak protest; at least she thought it was a protest. But even to her own ears it sounded like a sigh of need.

And Jack, the cad, took it for one. He kissed her again until she was boneless, brainless, melting against him like butter. He nibbled on her lower lip, tempting, teasing, until she gasped with want. His arms felt so good around her, like they were something she vitally needed, would die if she didn't have them there.

But this she knew was crazy. Jack was the last man on earth she needed, the last man on earth she dared trust with her

139

heart. She managed another sound of protest, this one a little more convincing, and pushed him an inch or two away. "Jack Murdock, remind me never to trust you around a fortune cookie again."

She was glad it was dark outside and he couldn't see how much his kisses had unhinged her. Getting into the MG she struggled to gather her wits that Jack had scattered like pebbles.

This time when she made herself a promise never to kiss the man again, she intended to keep it.

Jack felt like he'd been struck by a passing semi after that kiss. He'd dropped Holly back at her car, watched her safely drive off toward home, then headed home himself.

Alone.

So he wasn't tempted to repeat the kiss that had sent him reeling.

When he reached the ranch he didn't want to go indoors. The walls wouldn't be able to hold his rioting emotions. Not tonight. Holly had him turned inside out with wanting her.

He had no idea where this whole thing was taking him. Taking *them*. He was as dazzled by this woman as some high school nerd who found himself love-struck over the pretty head cheerleader.

Besides, he wouldn't get any sleep tonight. Holly would have him tossing and turning until daybreak. And that wasn't good. He had to be on Mad Jack's lot early tomorrow, preferably with a clear head or he could end up losing a profitable sale.

Damn, but he had it bad. He had to get a grip, or his life—and Mad Jack's—wouldn't be worth a plug nickel. He strode across the drive to the stables, checking on his horses, making sure they were all okay. He wanted to buy more when he

140

could spare the cost. He intended to add cattle soon. Then his ranch would begin to feel like a real ranch—and hopefully begin to turn a profit.

He sauntered over to the corral and sat on the top rail, his heels hooked on the bottom rung. He remembered their day together on the ranch, her kisses, and the touch of her fingertips on his hot skin. That, fueled with her kiss tonight at the restaurant, had his libido tied in a virtual knot.

He gazed at the night sky. The stars were bright, though the moon was partially obscured by a passing cloud. Everything was silent—something he didn't get much of back in New York.

He'd wanted to buy the ranch, had wanted to try his hand at something new, but he hadn't intended to get himself tied up in knots over some woman.

No, not some woman. Holly.

Just Holly.

Jack had always been good at making money, but what did he know about relationships? *Real* relationships? A lot less than he knew about running a Texas ranch. A whole lot less.

He admitted to himself that he wanted to get Holly into bed, but beyond that . . . ? Where was this thing between them headed?

He couldn't see himself doing the marriage thing. And his mother already had plenty of grandkids to dote on. She didn't need Jack to produce a few more. His sisters, Julie and Janet, had taken care of that.

In truth, he'd never felt a strong need to settle down. Hell, he was still figuring out his life. Holly, on the other hand, knew exactly what she wanted from life, making Hanford's a success. How did she feel about love, marriage, and children? He doubted she considered any of them. She'd been dealt a boatload of pain, if his guess was right. Men didn't rate high on her list of people she trusted.

Maybe he should back off, just work the ranch, make a tidy little sum on Mad Jack's, then take whatever came next in his life.

Even if that wasn't Holly?

To Jack, that was the rub.

Whenever he thought ahead to what came next, Holly was always there.

Chapter Ten

If dealing with her shaky emotions over Jack wasn't trouble enough, Holly encountered even more the following morning when she arrived at work. The attorney she'd heard from earlier had called again, increasing the bid for Hanford Motor's to an even more phenomenal amount.

Holly reassured the man that she wasn't interested at any price and told him not to contact her again. She hung up the phone and paced her office.

A call from an attorney with an anonymous buyer for Hanford's, then a rumor that could easily sink her business, and now this second offer? What was going on? Who was behind all this?

And what was she going to do about it?

Holly had no answer to the questions, and wearing out the plush blue carpet in her office wasn't going to give her any. She reached for the phone and called the one man who might be able to help her—Brewer Phillips, her long-time friend and mentor. She hadn't heard from him in several weeks and found she missed their talks immensely.

Brewer answered on the second ring.

"I'm looking for a handsome man to take me to lunch today," she said to her good friend.

"Flattery will get you everything, my dear," he said with

his usual good-natured laugh. "And I just happen to be free. How about the Tumbleweed Café at noon?"

It was a restaurant they patronized often and Holly agreed. "See you then," she said.

She tried to fill the rest of her morning with paperwork, but she couldn't concentrate on a thing. She studied the clock, rearranged the paper clips in her desk drawer, and sharpened every pencil she could find. These were not the actions of a successful businesswoman, she thought. Next she'd be playing solitaire on her office computer.

Business had been way off this past week. Several of her salesmen were threatening to leave for more lucrative positions—and Holly was sitting here counting paper clips in her desk drawer.

What was happening to her life?

It was quickly turning into one she didn't recognize.

She opened her bottom desk drawer, retrieved her purse and headed for her car parked at the side of the building. She'd be early for her meeting with Brewer, but if she hung around the office another moment more she'd go crazy.

Out of habit she glanced across the street, but saw no sign of Jack. But even the fact that he wasn't there, making sales hand over fist, didn't allay her nerves. It was probably just a lull in his activity. Holly's lull could quickly become permanent.

She got into her Thunderbird and headed toward the restaurant. Was Jack behind what had been happening to her? Or was he the innocent man he claimed to be? Holly didn't have the answer to either question, just a long string of suspicions.

And doubts.

She arrived at the restaurant and found a back booth where she and Brewer could talk quietly. The waitress had just brought water glasses and menus when she saw Brewer coming through the front door.

She waved him over.

"How's the prettiest woman in town?" he asked and gave her a quick peck on the cheek.

Holly gave him a welcoming hug and sat back down in the booth. "I'm afraid I'm not very good right now," she said.

Brewer studied her face for a lengthy moment. "What's going on? I've never seen you look this worried. Not even the day you opened Hanford's as your own baby."

Holly choked back tears, realizing what she longed to do was take her huge burden and place it on Brewer's wise and capable shoulders, but she knew she couldn't do that. The problem was hers and hers alone.

But Brewer was a man she could trust; he knew this business—and she could rely on his insights and opinions.

"I leaned on you a lot in those days, Brewer, and I'm afraid I need to do so again. Or at least seek your sage advice."

His look was gentle, concerned. "Anything, Holly—you know that."

Holly sighed, feeling better already. They ordered, and while they waited for their food, Holly filled him in on what had been happening at Hanford's, the rumor about her place, the offer from someone wanting to buy her out.

His face grew dark as he listened, stopping her only once to clarify. "This lawyer—he won't reveal the name of his client?"

"He says it's a blind offer."

His eyes narrowed. "I hope you told him where he could put his blind offer."

Holly gave a small smile. "I did, but in polite words. I can handle the attorney, I think. It's the rumor that has me worried."

"Worried? I'd be royally furious. I'll ask Brad if he's heard anything," he said. "He hasn't mentioned anything to me, but then he's trying to be his own man these days."

"How's he doing?" she asked.

Brewer looked suddenly tired, distressed. "Unlike you, Brad doesn't appreciate my humble advice."

"That's too bad, Brewer. You're a font of good advice."

Their food arrived and both of them were silent until the waitress left. Then Brewer looked over at her. "Do you have any ideas, any suspicions about who might be behind this?"

Her forehead pleated in a frown. "Only Jack Murdock."

"Ah—yes, Jack," Brewer said, then studied her for a long moment. "Holly, I know he's caused you a lot of headaches, moving in across the street from you, but I can't see him doing something like this. He's an okay guy in my book."

She felt a quick stab of betrayal. "Brewer, you can't mean that."

"I do."

Holly had a hard time recovering her usual aplomb. "How can you say that? The man is outrageous. Haven't you seen his horrible TV ads—not to mention those *ugly* jackets he wears?"

"It's called showmanship, Holly—and it gets him noticed. It brings in the buyers. His is a start-up business and the man wants to succeed, so he pulls out all the stops."

"Including starting rumors about my business and trying to buy me out?"

Brewer shook his head. "I can't see the man doing anything like that. I suppose I could be wrong about Murdock, but I don't think so, Holly. I'm a pretty good judge of character."

"I know." She'd give Brewer that. But she had her doubts

about his opinion this time. She wasn't at all sure Jack could be trusted.

"Maybe I shouldn't say this, Holly, but I noticed that boy's pretty besotted with you. That gaze of his follows you everywhere."

Jack was no boy. As for besotted—Holly didn't believe that. He just wanted her to fall for his charm the way every other woman in the universe did. Something Holly refused to do. At least, *most* of the time.

"Maybe you should have your vision checked, Brewer. Jack Murdock is besotted with only one person. And that person is himself."

Brewer gave her a wry smile. "Maybe. Maybe not. But back to what we were talking about. Is there anyone else who might wish you harm? If it were me, I'd be looking at someone else."

"Such as?"

"An angry ex-employee maybe. What about Adam Stone? You two didn't part on the best of terms, as I recall."

Adam. Jack had suggested the same thing. She mulled this over for a moment. "I suppose it's possible—but Adam left town a long time ago, Brewer. I haven't heard from him since. I don't even know where he is."

Brewer nodded. He'd finished his burger and was now munching his pickle chips. "What about someone who's still around, like T.R.? Have the two of you had any disagreements that run deep?" he asked.

"None. In fact, I'm afraid I'm going to lose him to another sales job if business doesn't pick up soon."

T.R. was loyal to a fault. She refused to think it could be him—or any of her other employees. She treated them fairly and honestly and they knew it.

Losing them because of a lack of business was something

else. She couldn't expect them to hang around and watch Hanford's go down to defeat.

"I've got to admit I'm baffled, my dear—but I'll nose around, see what I can find out. Between you and me, this retirement thing stinks. The fish haven't been biting worth a darn. I need something to make me feel useful again."

"You're useful to me, Brewer." She reached for his hands across the table and squeezed them warmly. "And thanks for your help. I know I can always count on you."

Holly tried to pay the tab, but Brewer refused. "At my age, it's nice to have a date with a beautiful woman."

"Be careful, Brewer. Your charm is beginning to sound like Jack Murdock's."

Brewer grew serious as they went to leave. "Why don't you give that poor guy a break, Holly?"

Give Jack Murdock a break?

If she did, he'd have her in his bed in no time. And that would be danger—the kind she didn't need.

Over the next week Holly's sales continued to slide and Jack's went up proportionately. Just the sight of those banners of his, flapping in the warm summer breeze, and his ugly sign lit up for the whole world to see, put her in a huff.

She just wished she could find out who was behind the rumor—and how to combat it. She wanted to climb the flagpole out in front of her place and shout to anyone who would listen that Holly Hanford was honest. But she knew she'd only come off looking like a madwoman. There was nothing she could do but wait for everything to die down.

And hope she was still in business when it did.

This morning, she had arrived at the lot early. She wanted to go over the books and see where she could cut expenditures. She refused to reduce salaries or commissions for her employees. They didn't deserve that. They worked hard and did a good job. She had to find another way.

Holly clicked on the lights in her office, put her purse away in her bottom drawer and set to work on a belt-tightening budget plan. Brewer had asked around about the distressing rumor and had called her yesterday to tell her that he hadn't uncovered anything yet, but was still on the case. It was the most she could ask. He'd suggested she retrench financially until the dust had settled.

Not exactly what she wanted to hear—but it was advice she was taking. Brewer was levelheaded; he'd been through about everything there was to go through in the business. And he'd never steered her wrong before.

Midmorning she glanced up from her paperwork to find Jack standing in her office doorway. He looked as tempting as ever in his dark jeans and pearl gray shirt, his tie slightly askew. At least he wasn't wearing one of his ugly jackets today. Though she'd probably have been better off if he was.

"If you've come by to gloat over your busy lot, I'm not in the mood to listen," she told him. "So just go away."

"My, but we're in a touchy mood." He leaned against the doorjamb, looking as handsome as the devil himself—and twice as dangerous.

"You would be too, if your sales record looked like mine this week." It hurt her to admit it—and to her archenemy, at that. But the man had eyes. He could see that barely a car had moved off her lot.

"I noticed business hasn't been too brisk over here this week."

That was the understatement of all time.

"Look, Holly . . ." He pushed his way into the room and took a seat on the corner of her desk. "If you're over-inventoried, I can take a few vehicles off your hands. I'm not sure I can handle many, but I'll do what I can. If it will help."

Holly met his gaze, waiting for a sharp barb or a gloating smile, but none came. Jack was serious about his offer. "I'm holding my own right now, but thank you," she said. "I hope I don't have to take you up on it."

He pushed himself up from her desk. "Well, back to the salt mines," he said and then he was gone, leaving Holly wondering why he was being so nice.

Over the rest of the week Jack kept an eagle eye on his competitor's business. Holly had had a few customers— which was more than he could say about her previous activity. How long could she go on at this rate? He was the financial genius here but it didn't take a genius to know what would happen. Holly's sales would continue to slide until she could no longer keep her business afloat. Then the bid made for Hanford's would begin to look good to her.

Only the deal the attorney would propose would be far less than the original, Jack was sure. And Holly would be forced to take it.

Jack couldn't let that happen.

He meant his offer about taking some of her inventory off her hands. But that would only slow the hemorrhaging, he knew, it wouldn't stop the bleeding.

Who would stand to gain from her defeat?

Besides himself?

But Jack wasn't the one Holly had to worry about. There was someone out there intent on doing some damage to Hanford's, or barring that, to buy her out.

Jack was just about to close up shop for the day when there was a rap on his half-open office door. He glanced up and saw Brewer Phillips. He stood up from his desk and shook the man's hand. He liked Brewer, and had heard through the grapevine that he was doing a little sleuthing on Holly's behalf. Jack had been wondering when he'd get around to quizzing him.

"Have a seat." Jack offered one fairly battered chair and Brewer obliged. The man was looking good; retirement must be treating him well. "I think I know why you're here, Brewer, and I just want to say I'm not involved in any of these things that have been happening to Holly."

Brewer gave him a long steady gaze as if evaluating the truth of his statement. Finally he spoke. "I thought as much. But I needed to have you look me in the eye and say it. Actually, you're the last man on my list of suspects, which is why I haven't been by about this sooner."

Jack let out a slow breath. "Well, it's refreshing to hear I'm last on *someone's* list because I'm *first* on Holly's."

Brewer gave a low chuckle. "I'm sure of that."

Jack opened his bottom desk drawer and pulled out a bottle of good bourbon. "Can I interest you in a little nip?" he asked Brewer.

"Don't mind if I do," the older man said.

Jack produced two paper cups and poured a little in each, then handed one to Brewer. "Excuse my fancy glassware," he said with a laugh.

"This is good enough. I offered many a drink to customers in cups just like this." The man took a slow swallow and a smile wreathed his face. "Good stuff, Murdock," he pronounced.

"Thank you." Jack leaned back in his chair and put his feet up on one corner of his desk. "I've been meaning to have you out to the ranch one day. But I've been busy making repairs out there and also busy here, hoping to hold my own."

"I heard you had a nice spread. Ranching and car sales," Brewer said as if mulling over the incongruity of the two endeavors. "That's enough to keep a man busy."

"It is." Jack hoped the man realized that didn't leave much time for duplicity. But they were making small talk, when it was really Holly Jack wanted to talk about. He and Brewer were both worried about her—only Brewer she trusted. Jack, she didn't. "About my beautiful across-the-street competitor—have you come up with anything yet?"

Brewer shook his head. "Not a glimmer—but something sure as hell is going on. I don't like suspecting everybody and his brother; that's not my way. But it sure looks as if Holly's got some tough going ahead of her. Someone out there wants to cause her a peck of trouble and I don't know who that someone might be."

Jack wondered if Brewer had quizzed his son, Brad. The guy was new in the game, like Jack. How big a splash did he hope to make in the business? And would he resort to deceit to achieve it? Jack didn't like accusing anyone either and certainly not Brewer's own flesh and blood, but *someone* was sure out to cause harm to Hanford's, and Jack didn't want to leave any stone unturned. He'd do some low-key snooping of his own.

"Holly's refused my help," Jack said, "but I'd like to lend a hand any way I can."

"Good," Brewer replied. "And don't worry about Holly— the woman's stubborn to a fault, but she needs all the help she can get right now."

He got up to leave then, but at the door he turned back with a buttonhole glance at Jack. "You know Holly doesn't have a daddy to look after her welfare," he said, "so I've sort of appointed myself to the task. Might I ask what your intentions are toward her?"

"My intentions . . . ?" Jack swallowed hard, realizing Brewer wasn't referring to the trouble Holly was having with her business. On the contrary, Brewer meant something a whole lot more personal. "To be honest, the woman's turned me inside out," he said. "I hardly know up from down anymore. But I don't think she'd have me—unless it's my head on a platter."

Brewer gave a low chuckle, as if he might have suffered Jack's plight a time or two himself. "I just don't want you to go breaking her heart," he said.

"Trust me, Brewer, hurting her is the *last* thing I want to do."

"Good. She's been hurt aplenty in that department already. She doesn't need more pain and aggravation."

With that word of warning, he was out the door.

Damn, Jack thought. Now he had Brewer Phillips nipping at his heels. If he caused Holly one iota of hurt the man would nail Jack's worthless hide to the nearest tree.

How had he gotten himself in this pretty predicament?

A lot of the dealers in town chose the Tip Top Bar as a place to unwind after a full week of work. Jack had been like a dog on the hunt the past few days, trying to find out who might want to sabotage Holly and her business. But if someone in this town was spreading ugly rumors, Jack's detective work hadn't uncovered the offender. At least not yet. Tonight he intended to ramp up his level of detecting and do a little undercover work at the bar. Maybe after a few beers, tongues would loosen.

Brewer had admitted he was downright worried about what this rumor campaign could do to Holly's business. And if Brewer was worried, Jack was too.

He slid onto a bar stool and ordered a beer, then went in search of answers. Brad, Brewer's son, was in a back booth, along with a few other players in the town. The perfect person to target, Jack thought.

He didn't like Brad Phillips a whole hell of a lot. The man was arrogant—very *unlike* his father. Jack didn't care to socialize with the man or his cronies—but then he wasn't here to socialize. He was here to find out what, if anything, Brad and his friends knew about the rumor. Jack hoped for Brewer's sake, and for Holly's, that Brad wasn't the man involved.

But Jack had heard through the grapevine that Brad was jealous of Holly and only thinly disguised his animosity. His reason—that his father's help boosted her business and Holly Hanford was the competition. What Jack suspected though was that Brad didn't want to put out much effort to increase his business.

The group was loud, halfway to a good drunk. Brad saw him and waved him over. Jack pretended he was glad to be welcomed into the group so gregariously and took a chair on the fringes. He wasn't into downing beers and swapping tales, but these guys looked like easy pickings for learning gossip.

All Jack needed was a name.

"Howz-it goin', Murdock?" Brad asked him, speech tipped toward slurred.

"I'm a little behind you guys," Jack said, raising his beer like he intended to catch up to their drunken level soon.

Someone slapped him on the back. "Selling any cars, buddy?" the man asked him.

Jack knew the little weasel. He worked for Brad, hired on after Brad had taken over for his father. "One or two," Jack said, downplaying his quite profitable week. "How about you?"

The man looked glum. "I'm drinkin' my profits," he said with a self-deprecating groan.

"Tough, buddy." Jack raised his beer as if he understood.

The group ordered another round of drinks and Jack joined in. He could hold his beer. He wouldn't slip into inebriation. He popped some salted nuts into his mouth and spent the next quarter hour listening.

Brad was holding court, expounding on how he was going to outdo his old man's sales record, institute changes, and raise prices wherever he could. No more good deals for chump customers, that was Brad's new motto. A real principled guy. Jack was damned tempted to bust him in the chops for his arrogance and blustering, if not for his total lack of integrity.

Brad wouldn't be winning friends and influencing people with that as his ideal. What about spreading rumors about fellow players? Jack wondered. Where did Brad draw the line on honor and reputation?

A few more rounds of beers and Jack still hadn't heard what he hoped to hear from the group, like who in this town was spreading the hurtful rumors about Holly. The boozing was getting to him. So was Brad's unpleasant remarks about his father. The man had been handed the business on a silver platter and didn't have the graciousness to appreciate it—angry instead at Holly.

The evening was getting late and a band was warming up for their late-night gig. "These guys any good?" Jack asked Brad, indicating the band. Brad's pals had tripped off either to the restroom or to have a cigarette and they were alone.

"Who? What? Oh, the band. Hardly listen to 'em," he offered.

Jack slouched and tried to look aloof, bored, before posing his next question to Brewer's poor excuse of a son. No more playing footsie. Jack wanted answers. "You know anything

155

about these rumors going around about Hanford Motors, Phillips?" he asked, his gaze firmly trained on the man.

He didn't want to miss even a flinch on the guy's face.

But Brad only looked . . . drunk.

Damn, he thought. He may have waited too long to get a straight reaction from the guy. But he'd play out his hand, anyway.

Brad glanced up, eyes bleary, trying to focus on Jack. "You askin' me if I'm the one spreadin' 'em?"

"Yeah—I am," Jack retorted.

Brad took another long swallow of his beer. "Well, I ain't the one—but if you ask me, she's as guilty as sin. And givin' the rest of us a bad name."

Jack was out of his chair in a flash. He grabbed Brad by the shirt collar and yanked him from the booth. "Listen, you damned know-nothing prick, you're not worthy of having your name even mentioned in the same breath as hers." Brad's eyes bulged and Jack squeezed harder. "And if I hear you're involved in this in any way, you better be looking over your slimy shoulder because I'm coming after you."

He shoved Brad's miserable body back in the booth where it landed in a heap. "And I suggest you learn a little respect for your father, you ungrateful little bastard." As an afterthought he snatched up the man's car keys. "You can pick these up from the barkeep when you sober up."

Brad's eyes blinked wildly, and if the guy wasn't stone cold drunk Jack was sure he'd be coming after him. Instead he lay sprawled in the booth like the dirt bag he was.

Jack strode over to the bar and tossed Brad's keys on the counter. "Call my friend over there a cab when he's ready to leave," he told the bartender. He peeled off a few bills and tossed them beside the keys for the fare.

Scratch Brad Phillips off the suspect list, he decided as he crawled in behind the wheel of the MG and headed for home. If Brad had started any rumors he'd be crowing about it—but that didn't mean he wouldn't take advantage of Holly's situation.

Chapter Eleven

Instead of driving into her own lot Monday morning, Holly pulled into Jack's. He was showing an SUV to a customer but she could wait. She'd told him to stay out of her business, that she fought her own battles. Instead what did the man do but strangle Brewer's son half to death.

Brad had been hopping mad when he'd finally sobered up. Brewer had said the kid deserved it, sticking up for Jack's actions, which only incensed Holly even more. Brewer was her friend—and Jack had no right to get into a fight with Brewer's own flesh and blood.

And certainly not on her behalf.

She got out of the Thunderbird and stood beside it tapping her toe, arms crossed, ready to do battle with the man. She hoped he lost the sale he was trying so hard to negotiate. It would serve him right.

He spotted Holly and waved, motioning to her that he'd be right there. If he knew how mad she was, he'd be heading for the hills instead of trying to join her.

Finally Jack left the guy checking out the SUV and came over to Holly. "Good morning, beautiful, what brings you here so bright and early?"

"Don't *beautiful* me, Jack Murdock."

The corners of his sexy mouth lifted. "Okay, tell me

what's got your dander up?"

"Brad Phillips," she informed him.

"Ah, yes—well, the little pipsqueak deserved it."

She stabbed a finger at his big broad chest. "It doesn't matter whether the man deserved it or not. I told you I fight my own battles, Jack Murdock."

He smiled. "I'm sure you'd have choked the little weasel yourself if you'd have been there, sweetheart, but you weren't. I was just defending your good name."

"Don't *sweetheart* me either," she shot back at him. "And did it ever occur to you that you were damaging my good name by starting that brawl in the first place?"

He raised an eyebrow. "Who said it was a brawl? Brad and I just had a . . . minor difference in viewpoints."

"Don't try to soft soap it, Jack. And don't try to help me, either." She jerked open her car door and slid in behind the wheel. Jack Murdock was an aggravation she didn't need. She put the car into reverse, turned the wheels and sped off his lot.

"Is she one of your satisfied customers?"

Damn, Jack had forgotten the man looking over the SUV. He gave the guy a reassuring smile. "No—more like a woman who'd like to knock my block off. What did you decide on the SUV?"

His gaze followed Holly off his lot and across the street to her own. She'd been plenty riled up, but Jack didn't regret his clash with Brad Phillips. Next time he wouldn't go so easy on him.

The man decided on the SUV, talking Jack down on the price. Way down. But Jack's heart just wasn't in the sale. His mind had been on the red flush that decorated Holly's cheeks when she was angry, the way her eyes sparked jeweled green fire. Jack would no doubt have sold the SUV for ten bucks if the guy had argued the price down that far.

He wrote up the sale and sent the guy on his way with his new set of wheels. So he'd taken a bath on the deal. It was only money. He glanced across the street but didn't see Holly out on her lot. She'd love knowing he'd been rattled enough to practically give the SUV away.

Jack hoped the word didn't get out.

Holly was still furious at Jack when she reached her office. She closed the front blinds with a snap, not wanting to see, or even think about him for the rest of the day. She had work to do, a business to save from the clutches of red ink. Her belt tightening aside, the company needed every bit of luck it could garner.

At least she had lookers on the lot again, which was more than she could say about the week before. Her sales crew was no longer sitting around, looking bored. They had something to do. She hoped this was a sign that Hanford's had weathered the worst of the rumor with only a few minor bumps and bruises.

Holly had just finished a quick lunch at her desk when T.R. popped his head in the door. "We've got a guy out here interested in the Karmann Ghia," he said. "He wants to know what kind of price you want for it?"

"Are you serious, T.R.?"

He smiled. "I am."

Holly took a deep breath, barely allowing herself to get excited. It was a sale she could use—desperately. "Tell him I'll be right out, T.R."

She smoothed a wrinkle from her skirt and headed for the showroom. There she found the potential buyer looking over the car. "I understand you might be interested in the

Karmann Ghia," she said, extending her hand to him and offering her best smile. If charm worked for Jack, Holly wasn't above using a little herself.

"Yes, I'm somewhat of a collector and if the price is right I might be interested." He shook her hand. "George Samuels."

"I'm Holly Hanford, Mr. Samuels."

"Hanford? Then you own this place."

Why were people always surprised to find a woman in charge? She gave him a smile. "Yes, I do."

Holly told him the price she wanted for the car, hoping it wouldn't frighten him away. It didn't seem to.

He asked several questions about it, explained that he was from Tulsa and was an avid fan of classic cars. Like Holly, he had to enjoy the hobby on a shoestring.

And he was definitely interested in the car.

Holly explained how she'd come to buy the little classic, some of its history, its owners, the work done to restore it. It was a very good deal at the price Holly wanted for it. Mr. Samuels agreed. But he didn't seem sold.

"I'm afraid my wife has me on a pretty strict budget. She thinks I should find a cheaper hobby—like collecting arrowheads or fruit jars."

Holly had to laugh. "Is your wife in town with you?"

"If she was I wouldn't be here looking at the Karmann Ghia," he admitted.

The man didn't look like a henpecked male—but Holly understood. A lot of money could be spent on this hobby.

"I might consider buying it if we could reach some sort of compromise on the price," Mr. Samuels suggested.

Holly wasn't sure if she just wanted to sell the car or if it was because she liked Mr. Samuels. "Why don't we step in my office and discuss it," she said.

The man gave the car one long considering glance, ran his

hand over his jowls as if thinking long and hard over his circumstances. "Yes, let's," he said finally.

Holly led the way and ushered him into a comfortable chair in front of her desk. Mr. Samuels had the look of a well-heeled rancher, judging by his expensive hand-tooled boots and the pearl-gray Stetson he wore with the ease of a man well used to western headgear. She was sure that was a Rolex watch she saw peeking out from the cuff of his shirt. "What sot of price did you have in mind, Mr. Samuels?" she asked point blank.

"I like your frankness, Ms. Hanford," he said. "I'd bet you're an asset to your business."

Flattery might buy him a lesser price, Holly thought to herself. Still she had money invested in the little car and she had to consider that. They bounced price back and forth like a ping-pong ball for the better part of an hour. Holly picked up on certain nuances. First, the man really wanted this car. Second, he could afford it. And third, he had a wife to placate.

At another time she might have played hardball with him but a sale could greatly boost Hanford's bottom line. She considered what she had invested in the car, what he wanted to pay and agreed to a compromise on the price.

"You're one tough negotiator," he said, standing up and shaking her hand. "But I gotta say you're fair-minded. Now if the missus doesn't light into my tough hide, I'll be a happy man."

"I'm happy too," Holly said.

"How did it go?" T.R. asked as the buyer left the showroom.

"He wants the car," she said, unable to keep the smile from her face. "I had to do a little negotiating, but we agreed on a price."

T.R. looked pleased. "We may have a sale or more on the lot, too, before the day is over."

"That's wonderful, T.R."

Maybe Hanford's downward spiral was over.

At the least it earned Holly some breathing room.

It was Friday night—and the annual barbecue given by the town for the local merchants. Jack had learned the event got started seven years before as a thank-you by the town council for keeping businesses up and running in McCallum and thus filling the town's coffers. As owner of Mad Jack's, Jack had earned an invitation. And he was looking forward to attending.

More to the point, he looked forward to *Holly* attending.

Though he wasn't sure she was speaking to him yet.

But he intended to change that. He'd just turn on that magnetic charm of his and he'd soon have her eating out of his hand. Well, maybe not. In fact, he was sure he had his work cut out for him where she was concerned.

The barbecue was being held on Mayor Gower's ranch and it looked like things were in full swing by the time Jack arrived. Beer and old Texas bourbon flowed freely. A country band played loudly and couples danced the two-step. At least those who weren't busy loading up plates with food. The outlay was immense and it all looked delicious. Jack would make the rounds of the tables soon, but first his gaze tracked the crowd for Holly.

He snagged a beer from one of several washtubs on the grounds, popped the top and took a slow swallow. Maybe she'd decided not to come tonight. If so, Jack would be mighty disappointed. He'd also be surprised. It looked like the owner of every store and business in McCallum was present and accounted for.

163

"Jack, glad you're here," Alex Dodd, the owner of the local tack store, greeted him. Jack had patronized his place, buying various things for the ranch.

"Wouldn't miss it," he returned. "Looks like quite a turnout."

"Try the food, man, before it's all gone," Dodd said, motioning Jack toward the heavily laden tables.

"Doesn't look like we're in danger of that happening," Jack returned. The food would hold. Jack was more interested in finding Holly.

Then he saw her. She was dancing with some cowboy who looked like he had two left feet and Holly was doing her best to keep her red cowgirl boots from being mangled. She was by far the most beautiful woman here with her silky brown hair swinging loose, her face lit with a smile for her clumsy dance partner.

She wore slim-fitting jeans that made her legs look a mile long and her backside cute enough to pinch—though if Jack tried that she'd probably deck him. Her white sleeveless blouse showed off her tanned arms and skimmed over her pert breasts.

"I'm headed back to the food line," Dodd said. "Sure you don't want a plate?"

But Jack's mind was on other things—like Holly Hanford.

"You can have my share," he told Dodd, his gaze not wavering from the sight of Holly. He took another slow swallow of beer and decided he needed to cut in. He set his beer aside and went to claim her.

"Sorry, pardner," he told the cowboy she was dancing with, "I believe this is my dance."

The man reluctantly released her and Holly fixed Jack with a frosty glower. "This is *not* the way to get back in my good graces, Jack Murdock."

He gave her a slow grin. "Sorry—but it looked like you needed rescuing. That cowboy was doing his best to ruin those pretty little boots of yours."

"Jack, I'm a big girl—in case you haven't noticed."

"Oh, baby, I've noticed." He held her at arm's length and studied her from head to toe.

Holly rolled her eyes. "Jack Murdock, did I ever tell you you're one despicable human being?"

"Often, sweet thing. But that's okay. I know you're crazy about me."

Holly was *crazy* to be dancing with this man. Sooner or later, she was going to tumble into his arms and into his bed. The man never backed off. No matter how furious she got at him, he had a way of making her forget.

He looped her arms around his neck and pulled her close for yet another dance. He looked good tonight, dressed in western garb, snug jeans, western snap-buttoned shirt and cowboy boots. It was hard to imagine he was once a Yankee. He melded in with the group as if he'd been Texas-born.

Her fingers tangled in his hair that lightly brushed the collar of his shirt. He felt so male against her, his body hard to her softness. With him, her boots were safe from being trod on, but not her heart.

The evening sun had dipped low and orange in the darkening sky and Jack tempted her senses. He drew back and smiled at her, a smile entirely too charming for his own good—and hers. He lowered his head and claimed her mouth in a tender kiss that ricocheted through her. He gave a low groan she felt against her lips. "I'm glad you came tonight," he said.

His tongue skimmed her lips and her breath caught at the light touch, snagging her senses more than any deeper kiss could have. Why did her brain turn to mush around this man and her hormones go wild? Jack was danger, had been from the first moment she saw him.

The song ended and Holly needed breathing room. She pushed away from him. "That kiss didn't mean a thing," she said. "I'm still plenty mad at you."

"You could've fooled me, sweetheart."

She gave him a glower and walked away from him. She hadn't eaten and the barbecue smelled delicious. Maybe some nourishment would make her forget the feel of that kiss that still thrummed through her body. She was determined to keep her distance from Jack for the remainder of the evening.

In the food line she chatted with some of the other merchants and dished up some of the super barbecue onto her plate. Mayor Gower was doing the honors at the food table and they shared a few words. "I'm looking for a safe used car for my grandson, Todd—something sensible," he said. "If I send him by, do you think you can fix him up with something?"

"Mayor, your grandson is sixteen. He isn't going to want a *sensible* car. He's going to want something sporty—and fast. But send him by and I'll see what I can do."

She often got asked to be the voice of reason for the town's teenagers when their family didn't want to play the heavy. Pinstripes on an ordinary auto sometimes convinced a kid he had a hot set of wheels instead of something more realistic. Maybe it would work with Todd.

But what pleased Holly more was that the mayor apparently had confidence in her car lot, and didn't believe the rumors that had been plaguing her.

"Thanks, Holly," he said, and heaped her plate with an extra stack of barbecue.

She found a picnic table and placed her plate on it, then went to get a beer. When she returned Jack was there, looking very much as if he'd been invited to join her.

"Mmmmm," he said, diving into his plate. "This is great barbecue. Have a seat, Hanford."

"I believe this *was* my seat. What are you doing here?"

"Enjoying, Hanford. Enjoying."

The man was infuriating. And there was little she could do to remove him from the spot. She'd have about as much luck doing that as she had removing him from his place across the street from her business. She slid onto her seat beside him, careful not to sit too close. The man had a way of stirring her senses even from a distance.

"I've noticed business has improved over at your place," he said after polishing off an ear of corn. "And did I see the Karmann Ghia leave on a flatbed trailer the other evening?"

"You know it did, Jack. You weren't hiding the fact that you were out there on your lot taking it all in."

"Just trying to keep an eye on my competition," he said. "What kind of money did you get for the car?"

"Enough—not that it's any of your business. I haven't forgotten how you drove the price of it up when I was bidding on it."

He gave her a wide smile. "And I offered to take it off your hands for what you paid for it."

He had, she remembered. "The less business I have with you, the better it is, Jack."

He gave her another smile, then went back to devouring the food on his plate. Holly finished as much as she could eat and pushed her plate away. The beer was icy cold and tasted good. She loved a good old-fashioned Texas barbecue.

"Uh, oh—don't look now, Jack, but Brad Phillips just arrived. And he doesn't look too happy to see you here."

Jack glanced up. "I'm not too happy to see him here either—but if he behaves himself, I won't rough him up again."

Holly groaned. "How big of you."

"Look, Holly, I don't like it when some little twerp bad-mouths people I care about."

"Meaning me? I told you not to fight any battles on my account. I can take care of myself."

"He badmouthed Brewer as well—and the guy needed to be taught a lesson." Jack shoved his plate away. "Want to go back for dessert?" he asked her.

"I don't have room for dessert, but go help yourself."

He did, coming back with a plate loaded with a variety of sweets. Just looking at the food would make Holly gain weight. But Jack wouldn't gain an ounce. Life wasn't fair.

Having eaten his fill, Jack swept up their plates and tossed them in the trash. Night had settled in and candles and lanterns had been lit, casting a soft glow on the party. "May I have another dance?" Jack asked.

"There are plenty of females here to dance with," she said, hoping he'd find himself another dance partner—and yet afraid he might. Jack muddled her feelings. One minute, she'd like him to drop off the planet and the next she wanted his kiss. What was wrong with her?

"I checked out the other females. You're prettier. I want to dance with you."

It was his charm, that crazy, zany charm of his that tore down her walls of anger, melted her heart when it needed to be stone. "One dance," she relented.

He reached for her hand and led her toward the dancers. Holly was worried for Jack as they passed Brad Phillips on the way. His expression was dark, his gaze following Jack.

But Jack gave him a wave as if they were old pals. "How's it goin', buddy?"

Brad continued his menacing glower.

"Doesn't it worry you that you've made an enemy?" Holly

asked him as they found a spot in front of the band.

He gave her a small smile. "You afraid for my welfare, Hanford?"

Holly would never admit to that. "He's likely to pummel the starch out of you one day."

His smile widened. "You *are* worried about me. That's . . . sweet."

"Don't go thinking that. I haven't told you whose side I'm on, Jack Murdock."

He looped her arms around his neck and planted his hands at her waist. Why was it that just his touch could make her senses crazy? His smile was her undoing.

"I can take care of myself in a fight, sweetheart. But Brad won't start anything. He knows he was in the wrong."

That was what Brewer had told her too, but still she was worried. Though Jack was probably right; he could very easily take care of himself. Not too many men would go up against his muscle and brawn.

Their one dance ended up being more like five and soon Holly forgot about Brad Phillips. All she was aware of was the music, the dark night with the stars overhead—and Jack. He held her close, proprietarily close. She marveled at how well they fit together, step for step, move for move. But then Jack was smooth—and at the moment Holly was under his spell.

"I need a breather," she said after the third fast song and tried to drag Jack away from the dancers, but he caught her hand as the band segued into a slow country ballad.

"No way, beautiful. I want to hold you close."

Holly didn't know what he'd been doing if those last dances weren't holding her close, but she soon found out he was quite capable of *closer* still. Awareness rippled through her as he molded her to his hard muscled body and they swayed together to the slow, rhythmic music.

He smelled of soap and masculinity and when he lowered his head to kiss her, Holly was lost. He tasted of barbecue and beer with just a tang of the sweet desserts he'd polished off earlier. But mostly he tasted of danger. Danger, if she let herself succumb to him.

But she didn't have a prayer's chance of doing that as his tongue teased its way past her kiss-swollen lips and sampled the inner recesses of her mouth. Holly could taste the hunger he was barely able to hold in check. Jack Murdock was a man on the move, a seductive move, and if Holly wasn't careful she'd find herself in bed with him before the night was over. And that would be folly on her part. Jack was not a man to be trusted. Not with her heart.

"I think the song ended," she said, her voice a whisper of her own need.

"Who needs music?"

She felt his smile against her lips as he angled her head for yet another devastating kiss.

Jack had had one enjoyable night at the barbecue, but all those dances and kisses aside, Holly insisted on going home alone. The woman shook him to his core, made him want her like he'd never wanted another woman before.

He was falling for her, falling hard.

But Holly didn't exactly want him in her life. She might kiss with pure seduction, hot passion there just waiting to be released, but she was determined to keep her heart intact—and men like Jack out of her bed.

So he'd ended the night with a long cold shower and tried his damnedest to forget the sweet want he'd tasted on her lips, forget the feel of her soft, pliable body against his heat, the emerald fire in her eyes, the dangerous smile that tilted at her lips.

Damn, but there'd be no sleep for him tonight. Jack knew when he was beaten. Holly Hanford wasn't a woman a man could get out of his system.

Not easily.

If ever.

Chapter Twelve

Jack didn't see Holly the next few days, except for a quick glimpse of her across the street. She'd had some activity on her lot, but it was still far from her usual. This morning he'd decided to surprise her with doughnuts from Krispy Kreme. In fact, he bought a whole box to share with her and her staff. With business at a low ebb, they could use a good turn.

And it might just put him in good favor with Holly.

Hey, a man could hope.

At least with box in hand, she wouldn't order him off her lot with one of her snide remarks about his new summer jacket. Okay, so maybe puce was a little garish, but if it brought in the customers who was he to complain?

Besides, he got a discount on the garment because no one in his right mind would be caught dead wearing puce.

Holly had once asked him if he'd used only the ugly crayons in his Crayola box as a kid. It was a gibe, but he loved tangling with her. Though these days he'd prefer any tangling with her to entail sheets—but Holly wasn't going to tumble to that.

He pulled into her lot, then braked sharply. "What the hell . . . ?" Jack could only stare in disbelief. Someone had tossed white paint on at least a dozen of her best cars.

He found a place to park the MG and went in search of Holly.

He found her on the lot staring dumbly at a scene she couldn't quite comprehend. He passed the box of doughnuts off to one of her sales crew. Not even Krispy Kremes could solve this problem.

"What the hell happened?" he asked, drawing up beside her.

She didn't answer for a moment, just stood there in shock. Finally she spoke, her voice low and bruised. "We found the vandalism when we got here this morning."

"Holly, I'm sorry. Have you notified the police?"

"T.R.'s doing that now." She pressed shaky fingers to her temples. "I don't suppose you know anything about this?" she said, skewering him with a hard glower. "Forget I asked. You wouldn't admit even if you did."

"Holly, you can't think that I would—"

"I don't know what to think, Jack. All I know is that some-one's out to do harm to me and my business—and I don't know who that someone is."

Well, it wasn't him—but he didn't know how to convince her of that. It hurt like hell that she didn't trust him, that she could think even for a minute that he could do something so low.

"I suppose it could be kids out for a lark—a random act of vandalism," he said, doubting it even as he said it. Still it was a possibility.

"This was no random act. This ties in with everything else that's been happening to Hanford's, and until I find out who's behind it, everyone's under suspicion."

Including him, Jack knew. "Look, Holly, I know you don't trust me, but I'd like to help, to look into this and see what I can find out."

Someone would be bragging about this—and when he found out who it was he'd wring the guy's neck for what he was doing to Holly.

"No, Jack. This is *my* company and *my* problem. I'll deal with it myself."

She turned and headed toward her showroom, leaving Jack staring after her.

Holly didn't want Jack meddling into her affairs. She would handle things—as soon as she recovered from this morning's trauma. There was little hope the police could do much beyond taking a report and maybe making a few extra pass-bys. No one did this for a lark. It was planned, a cold and calculated act.

As for Jack, even if she had complete trust in him—which she didn't—there was little he could do. She'd hire security to watch the lot at night. It would be an extra expense—and at a time when Hanford's could least afford it. But she had no other choice.

She had to find out who was doing this. She may have been in shock earlier, but now determination had taken over—and she wasn't going down without a fight.

Jack was no longer the only one on her list of suspects—but his name was still up there at the top.

The remainder of the morning was busy as she talked to the police, made arrangements to have the vehicles repainted, and hired a security firm to watch her lot at night.

When the police left, she closeted herself in her office, door shut and blinds, too. She didn't want to see Jack—or his lot—across the street. His day was business-as-usual, while hers was mired in fear, suspicion and defeat.

No—not defeat. Holly wasn't giving up. She intended to fight back. But how? How did she fight an enemy she couldn't see? The strikes against her came out of nowhere. She didn't know how, where or when they'd come again.

The one fact that continued to niggle at her was that all this started after Jack moved in across the street. She couldn't believe that Jack could do anything this vicious. Sure, he wanted to inflict as many headaches on her as he could, irritate her, keep her on her toes. But this?

She couldn't reconcile this act of treachery with the man Jack was.

T.R. had told her that Jack had brought in Krispy Kreme doughnuts this morning. Several of them sat on a paper napkin on her desk, but she couldn't eat them.

Fear and fury clotted her throat.

Would Jack throw paint on her cars in the dead of night, then bring her doughnuts the next morning? She didn't trust Jack as far as she could throw him, but she had to admit, this was over the top even for Jack.

By evening the damaged cars had been removed, the paved lot cleared of paint, and other cars moved into place. Insurance would cover a portion of the bill for the repairs, but her premiums would increase horrifically.

T.R. rapped on her still-closed office door, then opened it and poked his head in. "Sorry to bother you, Holly, but the security guard is here."

"Good, T.R.—send him in." She wanted to explain what she needed done and leave her home number to call if any unauthorized person dared show his face on her lot.

She only hoped the guy would strike fear into the heart of any vandal intent on damaging her cars. She smiled for the first time that day—but it was a smile that quickly froze in place when she saw the guard that the security firm had sent her.

Damn! The man had to be eighty if he was a day, bent with

age—and wheezing as if he was ready to draw his last breath. She shot T.R. a stunned glance, but he just gave her an eye roll behind the guard's back and quickly exited the room.

The coward.

She pressed her fingers to her temples. Could her day get any worse? If it could, Holly wasn't sure how. This guy couldn't frighten away a skittish cat—much less catch someone intent on doing damage to her lot.

"Excuse me a moment," she said to the guard and hurried off to find T.R.

"I asked for a security guard," she said when she found him. "And they send me an aging Barney Fife?"

"I know, Holly, but Bruiser was the only guy they had available on such short notice."

"Bruiser?"

T.R. gave a low chuckle. "That's the man's name."

"T.R., the only thing that man can bruise is his own nose from falling on his face in the dark."

He turned his palms upward in a helpless gesture, and Holly realized there was no use battering him with her dissatisfaction. It wasn't his fault.

"I'm sorry, T.R. I don't mean to complain to you. I suppose the guy is better than nothing," she said, then returned to her office.

And Bruiser.

If the man hadn't died in the meantime.

"Okay, Bruiser, here's the plan," Holly said when they were both hidden in the shadows on her lot. "I'll watch the fence-line for anyone sneaking over the top of it. You watch for anyone approaching from the street side."

Holly hadn't intended to be here tonight, but she knew if she wanted Hanford's guarded, she'd have to help the man out. He could have a heart attack just tottering across her lot. If he had to give chase, his grandkids would be attending his funeral.

And Holly didn't want that on her conscience.

She'd gone home, put on her darkest clothing so she'd be less visible, and returned to the lot just before dark. Now she and her security guard were settled in for the night. Thankfully the night was warm, but clouds scudded across the dark sky, blocking the moon and stars and threatening rain. Holly just hoped it held off until morning. If she had to spend a sleepless night on her lot with Barney Fife, she wanted it to be a sleepless, *dry* night.

The only sound she heard was the hum of cars racing along Woodland Avenue. Across the street Jack's place was dark except for the security lights, similar to her own. She never realized how eerie they made the surroundings they lit, creating light interspersed with elongated shadows. With a fertile imagination like Holly's they appeared ominous and threatening.

Of course, she had Bruiser here with her. The man had informed her he had a gun and that he was a crack shot. Somehow that didn't give Holly any peace of mind.

Sometime around midnight she caught movement at the back of the lot and her adrenaline shot up. Someone was climbing over the back fence. She could just make out the shadow of a man before he dropped to the ground on Hanford's side of it.

Catching her breath she gave the guard a jab in the ribs and was sure she woke him up. Some security. If she wanted to catch the perpetrator, she'd have to handle this herself.

She could barely see the intruder in the tricky play of the lights, but he was big. Holly would have to rely on the element of surprise if she was going to take him down. Armed with a trusty tire iron, she headed for the culprit.

Just then Bruiser came rushing up behind her. "Step aside, missy," he said, full of bravado. "Let me handle this."

The guy was old and doddering—probably on work release from the retirement home. And more danger than a help. "Ssshhh," she whispered. "He'll hear you."

Didn't the man know anything about doing surveillance?

Holly certainly wasn't about to let him go off half-cocked to take on the enemy. Someone would get hurt—and that someone would probably be him. Or Holly.

She should have left the man asleep.

Better yet, she should have sent him back to the retirement home.

The culprit had a flashlight. She could see its beam darting around her cars. What was the creep up to? Trying to decide which cars to vandalize?

Holly intended to get him before he did.

She motioned Bruiser to stay back and sneaked into a better position to see what she was up against. The guy was dressed all in black, skulking around her back lot. His shoulders were big and he moved with a stealth her security guard lacked. In fact, she could hear the man's joints creaking as he tagged along behind her, loaded for bear.

The interloper was in her sights.

She edged through the shadows toward him, ready to make her move. She slid into position between two cars, and as the guy neared, she raised her tire iron and swung it for all she was worth.

The next thing she knew she was locked in an embrace, her swinging arm behind her.

"Just what do you think you're doing, Nancy Drew?"

Holly knew that voice—and the sexy scent of the man who

owned it. "Jack! What are you doing lurking around my lot at midnight?"

"Doing surveillance—or at least I was until you tried to part my hair with that *weapon* of yours."

Just then the guard came lurching up, ready to take both of them out with his gun. Holly just hoped the security firm had the foresight not to send him out with bullets.

"Who's he?" Jack asked, hooking a thumb in Bruiser's direction.

"My security guard."

Jack choked back a laugh, then turned to the guard. "Okay, Hopalong, you can put your weapon away. I'm not the bad guy here."

Bruiser, loyal to a fault—his only good quality—kept the gun pointed at Jack while he sought confirmation from Holly.

She nodded. "It's all right," she said. "Jack's harmless."

Holly wasn't at all sure of that, but at least he hadn't come equipped with a bucket of paint.

"You can leave now," Jack said, "I've got the place covered for tonight."

Holly frowned up at him. "Jack, Bruiser is *my* security guard. I'll tell him when he can leave."

"Bruiser?"

She shouldn't have let that slip. She could see merriment dancing in Jack's eyes. There'd be no end to his ribbing now. Besides, the surveillance had been a total bust, starting with her Barney Fife security guard.

Her shoulders drooped. "Look, Bruiser, Jack's right. That's it for tonight. I really, uh, appreciate your help."

His wheezy chest puffed up and he tried to look six-feet tall. She was sure in his mind's eye he was—tall and tough and fearless. In truth, the man was a safety hazard.

He stuck his gun in the waistband of his pants, macho-style, and Holly sincerely hoped the thing didn't go off or he'd have more problems than just age and incompetence.

"If you need me again, give me a call," he said before swaggering off with his bowlegged gait.

"Where'd you find Dirty Harry?"

Holly gave Jack a dark look. She'd never live this down. "The security firm sent him over. He was the only one they had on short notice. And just who invited *you* to this little party tonight, I might ask?"

Jack gave her a slow smile. Holly looked sexy as hell in her form-fitting, black sleuth outfit. In fact, he couldn't take his eyes off her. He'd slipped over her fence, intent on hiding out behind one of her vehicles to catch the perpetrator.

How the hell was he to know Holly would be here with an over-the-hill security guard—her armed with a tire iron and the old geezer with an itchy trigger finger?

"I just came by to help—and from the looks of things, you needed it."

"If you're referring to my security guard, we had everything covered."

He looked down at the tire iron she'd tried to whack him with. "I hardly call that having everything covered. Damn, Holly, if Bruiser hadn't shot you first, the culprit would have hit you with your own weapon."

She huffed, her hands on those trim, sexy hips of hers. "Did I ask for your opinion?"

Damn, but the woman was stubborn. "No—but I'm giving it to you anyway. And whether you want it or not, you've got my help, too. Now I'm going to check the perimeter once, then I'll settle in for the night. You can either stick it out here with me or go home and get a good night's sleep."

"I'm not going anywhere, Jack Murdock. And in case you

haven't noticed, Hanford's is *my* company. *Yours* is across the street."

"Fine, then stay."

He'd hoped she would do just that, but it would be a long night and she'd had a major shock today. She should be home in bed—and he'd love to be there with her. But there was surveillance to do, he reminded himself.

He glanced at the tire iron still clutched in her right hand. "I'm going to check the grounds, and when I get back, try not to swing that thing at me again."

Holly would like to split his skull with it. In fact, she'd nearly done just that awhile ago. But how was she to know he'd come over her fence and be skulking around her cars?

Her arm still hurt from him twisting it behind her, but she didn't want to admit that. It would just be further proof that she shouldn't be out here playing like one of the big boys.

She should go home, crawl into bed and forget everything until morning. She was weary enough—but she wasn't about to leave things in Jack's hands.

How did she know he wasn't the culprit, and this was just some big act of his? The man was shifty enough to be guilty of anything. But down deep in her bones, she didn't believe Jack was the vandal.

And she supposed she could use his help.

She doubted she could take on someone bent on trouble and live through it—at least not tonight. Her energy was sapped. For one time at least, she'd allow herself to lean a little on Jack's willing shoulders.

She sank down, her back against the trunk of an old oak near the rear of her building, her tire iron resting beside her, and scoured the shadows for Jack.

He was nearly on her before she saw him.

"Everything's secure for now," he said and took a seat beside her.

"That's good," she said. "Maybe there won't be any more activity tonight."

"If there is, we'll be ready."

Jack looked sexy in the shadowy light—those shoulders she'd decided to lean on, strong and capable; his profile handsome and resolute; his arms ropey with sinewy muscles showing beneath his short-sleeved black polo shirt.

He'd drawn his legs up and rested his arms on his knees, eyes intent on the dark in front of them. His jaw bore a day's growth of beard, and she wondered for a moment how it would feel against her warm skin.

A shiver of want rippled through her.

"Cold?" he asked and put an arm around her.

She didn't want to admit to any shiver of desire so she nodded. But she wasn't sure Jack's arm around her was the safer of the two evils. She could smell his male scent, all Jack, all sexy—and it was doing a number on her senses.

She needed to keep her wits about her—and not just because some vandal might sneak onto her lot. She needed to keep her wits about her when it came to Jack. It was going to be a long night.

With temptation sitting right there beside her.

"I want to get this guy," she said.

"I do, too, babe. I do, too."

She liked it when he called her that, though she shouldn't. She hadn't forgotten the way he'd kissed her at the barbecue the other night, the way their bodies fit together when they danced. Jack was becoming ingrained in her life, not just as a rival, but in other ways as well—*dangerous* ways.

She trained her eyes on the shadows in front of her, her ears tuned in to any sound, but she saw nothing, heard nothing, other than the sights and sounds of a normal night, sitting beside a very sexy Jack Murdock on her lot in the dead of night.

His arm stayed around her, making her feel warm and secure. She snuggled into him just a little, leaning against the broadness of his chest. She was tired, weary inside and out from today's ordeal, and Jack was there, all warm and appealing.

Maybe, just for a moment, she'd let herself relax against that ever-present strength of his, allow her head to drift to his big shoulder. Before she knew it, she was asleep.

Chapter Thirteen

"It's nearly dawn, sweetheart. Wake up."

Holly squirmed against him and Jack had never felt anything so erotic in his life. A low groan slid from his throat as
she snuggled deeper into him. Her body fit so perfectly
against him, it took his breath away. He wanted to lean down
and kiss that sleep-slackened mouth of hers, had wanted it all
night.

Her lashes fluttered but her eyes didn't open. Her hair
tickled against his neck, soft and silky. He'd never known a
woman could look so provocative, awake or asleep.

She wriggled again, nuzzling closer and Jack was sure he'd
die from wanting her. He lowered his mouth to hers, just a
taste to slake his need, and she responded.

Liquid fire raced through his veins. She'd be mad as a wet
hen when she woke up and realized what she was doing—but
Jack just couldn't help himself.

Holly was pure temptation.

Her lips moved under his, hungry, eager, pliable and Jack
was hot. He gave another low groan. "Unless you want to
make love in the back seat of one of your cars, sweetheart,
we'd better stop this now," he said around that delectable
mouth of hers.

That woke her. She jerked upright and gave his chest a

hard shove. "Jack Murdock, we're doing surveillance."

"Is that what you call it?"

She glowered. "You know what I mean," she said and gave his chest another shove.

A short moment before she couldn't get close enough. "And just to set the record straight, sweetheart, *I've* been doing surveillance, *you've* been sleeping."

"I wasn't asleep. Well, maybe just for a minute or two." She ran her fingers through her sleep-mussed hair, trying to straighten it, but only succeeded in mussing it more.

Jack wanted to delve his fingers in it, pull her close and taste that delightful mouth of hers again. "It was more than a minute or two, but don't worry about it. Our guy didn't show."

She sighed. "I don't know whether to be glad or disappointed. I wanted to get him, have all this come to an end."

"I know, babe."

He stood up and helped her to her feet. He wanted to make love to her right here, had wanted it all night, but he'd kept hands off. The hardest damn night he'd ever put in.

"Come on," he said. "I'll see you home. Are you awake enough to drive?"

She nodded. "I'm fine. I'm awake now."

The cool night breeze had revived her, but she wanted to go back to where she'd been, ensconced against Jack's shoulder, his warmth. She'd shoved him away, but she'd liked his kiss. Her lips still hummed from it, and her body felt all tingly where she had leaned against him during the night.

The guy hadn't showed—but she didn't kid herself that he was through with her or Hanford's. He would try again—she just didn't know how or when.

Jack insisted on following her home, and Holly didn't argue. He had a way of getting what he wanted despite her objections. When they reached her house, she invited him in for coffee. She needed some desperately and she was sure he did too. The night had turned chilly out on the lot.

She plugged in her fancy machine that helped her face the day each morning, ladled in the amount for a strong brew and motioned Jack to a seat at her kitchen table. "I appreciate your help last night," she said, and realized she meant it.

She'd leaned on Adam, but he'd felt the proprietary need to take over, not just offer assistance. Jack had not done that. He'd given her a choice of staying on the lot or going home to bed. In a few hours she'd probably wish she'd chosen the latter instead of the former. But she had gotten *some* sleep—tucked in Jack's embrace.

"Anytime, sweetheart," he said, that overly-charming smile of his looking like the real thing.

Or maybe she wasn't fully awake.

She started to pour the brew into the cups, but Jack came up behind her. He planted a kiss on the nape of her neck, then turned her into his arms.

"Did anyone ever tell you how beautiful you look in the morning?"

She tried to tell herself this was one of his lines, but the naked look in his eyes made her believe this wasn't just charm at work here. If she had any lingering doubt about his sincerity, his kiss the next moment washed it away.

His mouth was hot and bold, and she felt her body meld to his as if they'd been sculpted to fit. His tongue dueled with hers, exploring, sampling, claiming her as his own. He rocked against her, leaving no doubt that he wanted her.

Her head issued a flash of warning that she was falling for the enemy—but wrapped as she was in Jack's arms, he didn't *feel* like the enemy. His hands slid up and under her sweater, cupping her breasts through her bra, then under it in one of his many smooth moves—and bare hands touched bare skin.

Heat shot through her and she knew if she was going to stop this she needed to do it now. Instead she wound her arms more tightly around his neck and drew his mouth to hers in a hot, seductive kiss.

The kiss had its intended effect. He gave a low groan of need. "Damn, woman, I've wanted you all night."

She smiled at his words. Holly wanted him too, had for a long time now, though she'd spent plenty of time denying it to herself and everyone else.

But right now, this minute, denial was impossible.

"The kitchen table or your bed, darlin'?" he asked, his voice low and tormented.

She wanted to make love with him, despite all the ramifications of that. Sex with Jack would sizzle—and things would never go back to the way they were.

"I'm tempted to try the kitchen table and not wait for the bedroom—but the thing has a shaky leg and would probably collapse beneath us," she said.

"Oh, babe—are you promising me wild sex?"

She gave him a shameless smile and took his hand and led him toward the stairs. Her heart was thudding so hard she was sure he had to hear it.

Clothes fell to the steps, some hers, some his—and they were nearly naked by the time they reached her bedroom. He touched her bare breasts, tracing their curves with hot fingers, then rasped his thumbs across her nipples.

Holly gasped as heat shot to her core, a strong pull, coiling low in her body, then she gasped again as his mouth followed where his fingers had been. Her hands tangled in his dark hair and she pulled him closer, loving the sensations that exploded inside her.

He left her breasts and kissed her mouth as his hands slid beneath the silk of her panties. "I want you naked, babe."

With the ease of an accomplished lover he slid them off, then stood back and took in her bare body. She should have felt self-conscious, but strangely with Jack she didn't.

"You are so beautiful." His voice was a raw whisper that rippled over her heated skin, and in front of Jack, she *felt* beautiful.

His eyes were dark with need, a deep sultry blue. She reached out and undid the snap of his jeans, then slid them down his long body. She hooked a finger under the elastic of his shorts. "I want you naked, too."

She heard his sharp intake of air and he caught her hand. "I'd better do this or everything will be over before we start," he said.

She smiled, feeling a certain power that she could affect him that way. Her gaze trailed over him, liking what she saw, from the shadow of a beard that darkened his jaw, to his broad furred chest and his . . . maleness.

He picked her up and laid her on the bed, then took her mouth in a hungry claiming kiss. Her senses went wild, taking in so many sensations at once—the taste of his mouth, the feel of his hands, the sound of his low growl of need, the male scent of him, full of power and male musk.

He kissed her breasts, first one, then the other, then trailed his mouth down her heated torso, lower, then lower still, nearly driving her mad. His hands lifted her bottom and he touched his tongue to her core, sending shivers of raw desire shooting through her.

Her legs parted, allowing him easier access to this very private part of her until she was nearly insane with wanting him. "Not yet, sweetheart," he said when she demanded he take her. "I want you good and ready."

She *was* ready, damn it.

He gave a slow chuckle and continued his onslaught until she shattered around him. *"Now,"* he said and pulled her on top of him, plunging his hardness into her.

He stopped for a moment, letting her adjust to him and getting his self-control in check, then he began that rhythmic glide. Holly felt the heat build in her again. Jack kissed her long and hot, igniting her senses. The feeling of him inside her was glorious, wild, exquisite and she knew she'd never be the same person again. Her hips raised to meet his thrusts, wanting all of him. Her heart raced. Her throat went dry. And her senses were ready to implode, shatter with desire.

That magic rhythm he'd begun, a rhythm as old as time itself, picked up in tempo. They both raced to that edge, feeling as if they'd die if they didn't reach it. Urgency increased, the need in her raged hot, then hotter still, until she reached that naked crescendo that she couldn't stop.

Jack sensed it and got there with her.

And both of them spiraled into a climax so powerful it spun the earth on its axis.

"Damn, woman—do you know what you do to me?"

She swirled her fingers through the crisp dark hairs on his chest. "I have a pretty good idea."

Jack had sensed her passion, had felt it simmering there just below the surface of all that fire and fury of hers. But the reality of it was so much more than he ever imagined.

He pulled her close and gave her a slow, lingering kiss. He hadn't come to Texas to fall head-over-heels for Holly Hanford—but that was just what had happened to him.

He needed a woman who could give him hell on a daily basis and have him coming back for more. Jack had it bad—

he knew that. And he also doubted if there was a cure for it.

"I think our coffee got cold," she said, as if it were an accusation.

"Yeah," he answered, "but it was worth it."

She snuggled in next to him and Jack cradled her in his arms. He felt his body stir again, wanting her, but if he stayed here in bed with her, he'd have her again and again until she wore his body out. In fact, he was beginning to think she'd done that already.

He sure as hell didn't have the energy to move.

"Come on—I'll fix us fresh coffee and maybe some breakfast to go with it," she said, sitting up.

The sheet fell to her waist, leaving her breasts bare to his gaze. His libido gave a jerk and he wanted to drag her back down to him and make slow steamy love with her. The sunlight streaming in through the window reminded him cruelly that they both had businesses to run sometime today.

"I'll do the coffee," he said reluctantly. "You handle the stove."

He pulled on his jeans while Holly found a pink shortie robe and tied the sash around her waist. His eyes trailed over her sexy shape the robe couldn't hide. The silky fabric hit mid-thigh, leaving her long gorgeous legs free to view.

Maybe he'd drag her back to bed after all, nudge the robe apart and delight in her again—but there wasn't time for that. He followed her down the stairs and into the kitchen instead, watching the sweet sway of her backside all the way.

"How do you like your eggs?" she asked, reaching to pull a carton from the fridge.

"I'm easy."

"I know that, Jack."

She turned to look at him. Dressed only in his jeans riding

low on his hips, top snap open, he looked devastatingly male.

And tempting.

She wanted to slide her hands around his waist and explore his body—though she'd done a pretty thorough job of that a short while ago. Her heart pounded at the memory, and her sated body wanted more of him.

Breakfast—she needed to keep her mind on what she was doing. "Pop some bread in the toaster," she told him as she found a bowl and started scrambling.

He did, and Holly's gaze trailed over his body, remembering how it felt aligned with hers, his heat turning her to liquid fire. She'd known it would be this way with Jack.

It was why she'd resisted so hard and for so long.

She poured the beaten eggs into the melting butter in the frying pan, turning them until they were light and fluffy.

Jack abandoned his toast-making duty and slid up behind her, nuzzling her neck. "You look so domestic in the kitchen. I'd have never guessed it, Countess."

"There's a lot you don't know about me, Jack Murdock."

"I'm sure—but it's going to be fun finding out." He kissed her neck again.

"Unless you want your eggs scorched, go pour us some orange juice." She threatened to swat him with her spatula, but he slid under her swatting arm and stole a kiss from her lips before crossing to the fridge to find the juice.

She wanted to call him back, wrap her arms around his neck and kiss him long and hard. She wanted to drag him up the stairs and make love with him again. But she shook off the impulse and slid the nearly burned eggs onto a platter. Jack could distract her like no man ever could—certainly never Adam.

He had the kitchen table set, juice beside their plates, toast buttered and fresh coffee poured. The scene was one of domesticity. Too much so? She'd stayed away from anything smacking of a relationship so long, but strangely with Jack, this felt right.

Right and wonderful.

But now was not the time to distract herself with Jack. She had someone out to do her harm, the remembrance of that jolting her back to reality.

"I hope you're going to get some sleep before going in to work," he said across the table.

"I had sleep, *some* anyway."

"Not enough, babe. I'm sure T.R. can handle things until later."

She set down her juice glass and reached for a piece of toast. "In case you've forgotten, someone's out to sabotage my business. I *need* to be there." She didn't dare let down. "Besides, I'm sure you've worked without sleep in that concrete jungle you used to work in."

Jack had—too many times. And then he'd burned out, took a long, hard look at his life, and found all he had to show for it was money. It wasn't exactly fulfilling.

He wanted something more.

Had he found it here in Texas—with Holly?

A woman changed things in a man's life—changed everything. "Look—I don't want to see you on that lot before one o'clock."

"Noon."

"One. You have to be the most stubborn woman I've ever met."

She gave him a smile as if he'd complimented her. And maybe he had. He certainly admired her determination.

He carried his dishes to the sink and washed them. Holly had finished her plate as well. He snatched it up, planted a steamy kiss on her lips. "I'll clean up the kitchen and let myself out. You go up and grab a little sleep at least."

He hoped he could sneak some shuteye himself.

One thing he knew for certain, he wouldn't get any around Holly.

It was nearly noon when Holly stepped into the shower. By twelve-thirty she was dressed and ready for work. Her mind tried to drift back to Jack and his lovemaking, but she needed to stay centered. She had a business to run.

Her lot was quiet when she arrived. She saw Jack across the street. *His* lot was not quiet. In fact, he looked busier than ever. When she walked into the showroom her salesmen were there idle, wishing for a customer, she was sure.

Holly had to turn things around—and soon.

T.R. broke loose from the group and followed her into her office. "How'd things go last night? Any trouble?"

"The culprit didn't show," she said, then a thought crossed her mind, one she didn't like. T.R. had known the lot would be guarded. In fact, he was the only one who knew.

Could he have something to do with this after all?

No. She couldn't let herself think that. She depended on him, considered him a loyal friend. She had to find out who was behind all this before she became suspicious of every-body.

"That's good. Did Deputy Dog work out all right?"

Her doddering security guard. At least T.R. didn't know about Jack. And what had happened between them. "Let's just say I had to help him."

"That bad?"

Worse, she wanted to say, but she didn't want to explain last night to T.R. Not about the guard—and definitely not what happened with Jack. T.R. didn't like Jack, she remem-bered.

And Holly? How did she feel about the man? Besides the fact that he was one fantastic lover. A small smile came to her lips but she quickly turned it off.

It wouldn't do to have the whole world know she'd made love with Jack Murdock.

When T.R. finally left Holly got down to work.

She called to line up another guard, hopefully someone capable of handling the job, but to her dismay Bruiser was the only one available. Holly didn't need that kind of headache. They promised her they'd have more guards available next week.

For tonight, at least, it looked like Holly would have to handle things. But she decided not to mention that to T.R.—to *anyone*. If the culprit thought Hanford's was left unguarded, maybe he'd show with paint in hand, and Holly would finally know who was behind all this.

It could be dangerous. Holly didn't know who she might be going up against—how big, how tough, how mean, that person might be. Or if he'd come armed with more than paint.

She didn't own a gun, nor did she know how to use one without shooting herself. She'd have to hope her tire iron would suffice. She intended to defend her business from whomever it was out to cause her harm.

Even if that person turned out to be T.R.?

Or Jack?

Or someone else she knew?

Whoever it was, she answered herself.

Holly sat in the big Olds at the back of her lot. She'd probably never be able to unload the behemoth. It looked like a small boat setting sail as it moved down the road, but the front seat was comfortable—better than the hard, cold ground she'd sat on the night before.

And tonight she didn't have Jack's warmth to lean into.

She didn't want the culprit to be Jack, didn't want to think he could do something so heinous—and then turn around and make love to her as if she were someone he cherished.

She could still remember the feel of him against her, the feel of him inside her—and probably would for the rest of her life. Jack had spoiled her for any other man.

But she couldn't think about that right now. If she wanted her life and her business on a steady footing again, she needed to find out who her menace was.

It would be a long night. Dusk had given way to dark only an hour before. Dawn was a long way off. In her mind she'd gone over all possible suspects, but was no closer to knowing who the villain might be.

Just then, she caught a glimpse of movement near the back wall. A glimmer of a flashlight, she was sure of it. Her heart thudded almost painfully behind her ribs.

What was she doing here? Could she really take on an unknown vandal without getting hurt?

This afternoon she'd thought she could, but it had been daylight then, and her courage meter had been set on *brave*. But in the dark that courage was floundering—big time.

She grabbed her tire iron tightly and quietly opened the car door. She'd deactivated the dome light earlier, so its beam wouldn't give her away.

Warily she moved toward the gleam of light.

She hadn't expected anyone to make a move so early—but someone definitely was. She moved stealthily forward, angling around so she could catch the guy from behind. She didn't want to meet him head on.

She took a few deep breaths, trying to slow her heart rate and its noisy rhythm. A lump was firmly lodged in her throat.

She took a few more steps, sticking to the shadows.

She could see him better now, flashlight in one hand and something in his other—something that looked suspiciously like . . .

A bucket of paint.

Her adrenaline surged, supplying her with a quick shot of that courage she desperately needed. She was just coming up from behind the beam of light when the culprit turned and aimed the flashlight directly into her eyes, blinding her and rendering her helpless.

He must have heard her approach.

"Holly, dammit—are you out here all alone?"

Jack Murdock!

Her heart dropped to her toes. "What if I am? And what are you doing with that bucket of paint?" She tried futilely to see around the beam of his light to the offending object he was holding.

"Bucket—? Damn, Holly, this isn't paint."

"Then, what is it?"

She kept her tire iron ready. The man was so slick she was sure he'd try to lie his way out of the irrefutable.

He raised it higher.

She raised her weapon in quick response.

No way was she going to allow him to toss anything on her vehicles—even if he was the man she'd fallen for in a fit of passion last night. Or rather, early this morning. That's what he was doing to her life. She didn't know morning from night, up from down. She only knew that somehow Jack had made her care for him. Against her better judgment.

He moved the beam from his flashlight away from her to the bucket in his hand, illuminating it clearly. But it wasn't a bucket. It was a basket.

"I figured you'd be just stubborn enough to try to guard

this place yourself so I came by to help. This evidence of my high crime happens to be sandwiches and coffee."

Holly lowered her arm. "Jack, I—I thought—"

"Thought I was your vandal."

How did she know he wasn't? She hated being this wary. But Jack could be clouding the issue right now with his gesture of caring to throw the suspicion away from him. How was Holly to know whom she could trust—and whom she couldn't?

This was driving her insane.

"This is my problem, not yours or anyone else's. And I'll get to the bottom of it my own way. Thanks for the gesture—but no thanks."

Damn—but the woman was stubborn. Jack ought to take his offerings and leave her to sit in the chill of night all by her lonesome—but he knew he couldn't. He'd worry about her, and wouldn't get a wink of sleep wondering if she was out here trying to take down some man twice her size.

She didn't know her own limitations.

He thought he'd broken through that shell of toughness when he'd made love with her. She'd certainly been soft and malleable in his arms, but tonight that toughness was firmly back in place.

"It may be your problem—but you can't take down some guy bent on trouble all alone. Whether you like it or not, you're going to accept my help. Now, come on, let's get this stakeout under way."

"Damn you, Jack Murdock."

She might not want him here, but she turned and headed toward the back of her lot, leaving him to bring up the rear. She looked slim and stealthy dressed all in black again—as he was. She stopped a row or two away from the back of the lot and opened the door to a dark-colored Olds.

At least she'd had the foresight to disengage the dome light. That was why he hadn't seen her until she was nearly on him. But then Holly was no fool.

She was bright and knew what she was doing.

However, she didn't seem to realize when she needed a man's help. Or she was too hardheaded to take it. Jack slipped in on the passenger side while Holly took a seat behind the wheel.

"The wind is chilly. I thought sitting here would be warmer," she said.

"Good move." Jack dug into the basket and pulled out a sandwich. "Ham and cheese. I bet you didn't bother with dinner."

"I had an apple," she said.

She was still as prickly as barbed wire. "That's not dinner."

She shot him a glower but took the sandwich, unwrapped it and took a bite. "Mmmm, this is good."

"That's the extent of my culinary skills—so don't get used to it."

She gave him a look that said that wasn't one of her worries. In fact, she looked like she'd as soon steal his food and coffee and dropkick him off her lot.

He supposed, given her mood, he was lucky she didn't.

He poured a cup of coffee for her and set it on the dash in front of her, then one for himself. He'd gotten very little sleep since leaving her this morning, and he hoped the caffeine would keep him alert.

"I'm sorry I came after you again with my tire iron," she said in a soft voice.

"Yeah, well, you have a habit of doing that."

"And you have a habit of sneaking over my back fence unannounced."

"If I'd told you I was coming, you'd have warned me away." He pulled out a sandwich for himself and took a bite. He was hungry, and he needed to keep up his strength if he was going to tangle with Holly.

The woman could test a man's endurance.

"I intended to have a guard for tonight but they only had Bruiser available," she said, reaching for her coffee cup. "Mmmm—the coffee's strong."

"Too strong?"

"No—it'll keep me awake."

"That was the idea."

They munched in silence for a while. Jack kept a wary eye out for their culprit, but the lot was quiet. The security lights offered up a hazy view of the place, and the traffic noise out front was muted.

The old Olds created a concealed cocoon for them.

"I'm going to check the perimeter," Jack said and slipped out the side door quietly. He also wanted to get the baseball bat he had stashed in the trunk of his car. He doubted Holly would relinquish her trusty tire iron, and Jack needed a weapon if things got hairy.

The sky had turned darker, with storm clouds moving in from the west. It would be the perfect night for the guy to strike if he was going to. He popped the trunk and retrieved his bat. He also grabbed the blanket in case their stakeout proved long, then made a circle around Holly's cars.

Holly felt the loss of warmth as soon as Jack left. Okay, so maybe she was glad to have him here. She had to admit, he made her feel more secure. Holly didn't know who the vandal was. If it was Jack, would he have shown up with sandwiches and coffee?

She didn't want to think so, but she was afraid for her

company. If things didn't turn around she'd soon be hanging out a Going Out of Business sign in front of her place.

She wrapped her hands around her coffee cup, liking the warmth to her fingers, and gave a wary glance around the lot. She couldn't see Jack. He'd blended in with the shadows. Dressed in black, as she was, he looked so tempting she couldn't keep her eyes off him.

But did she dare let herself fall under Jack's spell?

Again?

Just then the car door opened and Holly jumped, nearly spilling coffee in her lap. It was Jack. "You scared me," she said.

"Sorry about that." He gave her a slow grin. "What happened to all that bravery of yours?"

"I just wasn't expecting you back so soon."

He held her gaze for a moment.

"Okay. I admit it—I'm a little jumpy. Who wouldn't be?"

"Well, relax. No sign of trouble out there. I brought you a blanket. I thought you might be cold."

She set her cup on the dash and took it from him. "I am—a little. Thanks." She snuggled into the warmth. "Want a corner?"

"Honey, if I crawl under that thing with you, we won't get any surveillance done."

The sound of his voice was low and husky and it rippled over her. He was right, of course. They needed to keep their minds on the business at hand.

"Your weapon?" she asked, nodding at the ball bat at his feet.

"Hey—whatever works."

"Maybe no one will show. Maybe whoever's doing this has abandoned his plan."

"Is that what you think?"

"No—not really. I think he's still out there."

"I do, too."

That wasn't what Holly wanted to hear—but she was sure Jack was right. She tried to calm her anxiety and huddled under the blanket.

"Want a cookie?" he asked, opening up a small bakery sack of chocolate chips he had tucked in the basket.

"Maybe later." Right now she intended to just enjoy the warmth of the blanket and the security she felt with Jack here beside her in the ancient Olds.

She could have taken on the vandal alone. She was that determined—but she'd have been frightened to death doing so. And then there was the loneliness factor.

It would have been a long night without Jack.

Her heart trusted him—even though her head raised ugly suspicions. Her life was going to be a nightmare until she caught the real person doing this. Only then could her heart and head be in agreement.

She hoped the man showed his evil face tonight. She had to know the enemy she was fighting. She snuggled deeper into the blanket and let out a slow sigh.

At the sound, Jack glanced over at her. "Tired?" he asked. "We can take shifts if you want. You sleep awhile, then I will."

"This is *my* problem, Jack—and whatever happens tonight, I intend to handle it."

Even if she got hurt, Jack thought. It was why he couldn't let her do this alone. Holly was so damned stubborn she could be foolhardy at times. He recalled her passion in bed. Did she go after everything she did with equal passion?

He suspected that was the reality. The woman was full of heat and total determination. If she finally fell for a man, for *him,* it would be with that same tenacity.

Every man's dream.

He finished a few of the cookies just to satisfy his sweet tooth, then tucked the rest away for Holly. If the night went on endlessly, she'd be hungry later. He leaned back against the headrest, trying to relax, but his eyes remained vigilant—and his thoughts on Holly.

He needed to find out who was out to hurt her. He knew this slump in business hurt her financially—and if it continued she would soon be out of any options except to close down.

And that would crush her.

Success was part of who she was, the way his success on Wall Street had been to him. But Jack had wanted to stand for something more. He hadn't had to walk away in failure.

To Holly, failure would not be acceptable. Successful was how she defined herself. But successful was not the sum total of who she was.

She had brains and beauty, sophistication and a sense of fair play, people who loved her and so very much more.

But Jack knew that wasn't how she saw things. Part and parcel of having her business be a success had to do with keeping her father's business alive, the legacy he'd left her.

It also had been a part of her childhood and she loved it the way someone does a family home they grew up in. And Jack was determined to help her hang onto it—even if she didn't want his help.

Just then Jack saw something, a shadow of movement on the lot near the fence, movement so quick and fleeting he'd nearly missed it. Someone was there.

"Holly, I think we have company."

She sat up, alert, wary. "What? Where?"

"Shhh! Over there. By the fence. Stay quiet and stay put.

I'm going to investigate." He popped open the car door, but before he could get one leg out Holly had a death grip on the back of his shirt.

"Jack, this is *my* fight and I intend to be in on it."

He spun around and gave her a serious glower. "Holly, the guy could have a weapon."

"I have a weapon."

"A tire iron is no match for what he might have with him."

"And I suppose your baseball bat is?"

He gave a frustrated sigh. "Did anyone ever tell you you're one stubborn woman?"

"Often. Let's go."

How the hell had he managed to fall in love with someone so damned obstinate? But he knew that was just what was happening to him. If he had an ounce of luck, the trespasser would either shoot him or beat him over the head until he'd knocked some sense into him.

"Come on then, but stick with me—*behind* me."

It was a wonder they'd kept their war of words low enough the interloper hadn't heard them.

Being out here alone with her in the dark, armed with nothing more than a bat and Holly's tire iron, confronting a villain who could be armed with a knife or worse, a *gun*, had to be the nuttiest thing he'd ever done.

It ranked right up there with making love with her.

And wanting to do it again.

Hell, how was he going to protect her if the guy came at them with a weapon? He should have sent her home to bed— not that she'd have gone. She had more damned fight in her than a mother bear protecting her cub.

And she was just as dangerous.

The car door closed with a slight snick. Holly let loose of his shirt and stuck close behind him, matching him step for step, as they made their way toward the pale beam of light.

For now the guy was sticking to the shadows, so Jack didn't know what else he might have with him besides a flashlight dim enough to tell Jack it needed a change of batteries.

He needed to get a better look at the guy, see if he was armed. "Stay put right here a minute. I'm going to move in and see if he has a weapon," he told her.

She didn't answer him, and Jack figured if she did as she was told, it wouldn't be for long.

He edged forward and didn't feel Holly's body heat behind him.

That made him feel a little better for her safety, if only temporarily.

There—the man stepped out of the shadows, granting Jack a better look at him. He didn't see an open weapon, but he did see a bucket of paint.

This was their guy—and he was intent on doing damage. Again.

Jack jumped forward into his path, baseball bat hefted in the attack position. "Okay, pal—the game's up, put down the bucket and no one gets hurt."

Holly raced up behind the guy, having circled around behind, her tire iron at the ready. Obviously she hadn't stuck to his orders. True, they had the man cornered—but a cornered man was a dangerous man.

And Jack didn't want Holly in the line of fire.

"Who are you?" she demanded. "Why are you doing this, you . . . you lowlife?"

The guy gave her a quick glance as if she were nothing more than a biting mosquito. That was the creep's mistake, considering Holly little more than an annoyance. Jack remembered the swing she had with that tire iron last night and was just lucky he still had his skull intact.

"The bucket—drop it," Jack said when the man spun back around to face him. *"Now!"*

The guy hesitated only a moment, then hurled the paint at Jack.

Green paint.

Chapter Fourteen

Jack looked like the Green Slime Man from a Saturday morning cartoon show. The bastard must have run out of white—or maybe he just wanted to be colorful this time.

He wiped the paint from his eyes and saw that very little of the stuff had hit Holly's cars. Jack was the recipient of his latest hurl.

He also saw the guy had taken off, headed for the back fence.

With Holly in hot pursuit.

Jack jerked out his cell phone and dialed 911, giving his location and a terse summons for the police. Hell—he should have called for the cops the minute he caught sight of the guy.

If Holly got hurt . . .

He tossed the phone, leaving the connection open, and hotfooted it after the pair.

Holly had managed to hang onto the bugger's right leg as he attempted to scrabble over the fence. Jack was determined he wasn't going to get away. He reached the back of the lot in time to yank him down from his attempt at freedom, then applied a hammerlock the guy wouldn't soon forget.

"Okay, Picasso, who the hell are you—and why are you giving perfectly good cars a new paint job?"

He had a weasel face, with dark furtive eyes, the kind of

guy you'd find lurking in back alleys. He was short, no doubt the reason he had trouble scrabbling over Holly's fence. His clothes were dark and some of the green paint he'd tossed on Jack had spattered his black leather athletic shoes.

Jack would like to slime him with plenty more of the mess.

"Take it easy. You're hurting my arm," the man belly-ached.

Jack gave it another wrench for good measure. "Talk," he demanded.

The guy said nothing.

"Holly, do you know who this lowlife is, or why he doesn't want to talk to us?"

"I've never seen him before. But he's going to talk after I give him a hard kick in the family jewels."

Her chest was still heaving from exertion and probably from fury, as well—and Jack couldn't blame her. He wanted to kick the guy in the private sector as well.

"You heard the lady. She wants to hear you sing—and loudly."

Still the guy remained silent.

Holly didn't wait for him to decide to talk. She gave him a serious kick, strategically placed, and the guy doubled over in agony—or at least doubled as far as Jack's hammerlock allowed.

Jack gave her a slow grin. "Remind me never to get on your bad side, sweetheart." He jerked the bugger back upright. "Want another go at him?"

"*No!*" The little creep shrieked like a banshee. "I'll talk. Hell, this job ain't worth it."

Holly's head raised. "This job—someone *hired* you to do this?"

She felt a sick feeling in the pit of her stomach. Fear was

just now settling in, replacing the adrenaline that had sent her flying after the man.

"Turn me loose. I'll talk."

"Talk first," she said, "then we'll negotiate."

He stared her down with a heinous glower. "You drive a hard bargain, lady."

"She hasn't even gotten started yet, paint boy." Jack gave the guy's arm another twist behind his back.

"Okay, okay," the man squealed. His chest heaved and he kept a worried eye on Holly's kicking foot. "It was some guy—he hired me to damage the cars on the lady's lot and make trouble for her any way I could."

"Who? What guy?" Holly demanded.

"His name's Stone—Adam Stone."

Holly crumpled. *Adam?* How could he do something this foul, this heinous? And why? Did he hate her that much?

She knew he'd been bitter about their breakup, and the fact that she wouldn't take a backseat and let him run the business, but to go to these lengths?

Just then the lot was flooded with spotlights. Holly tried to peer into the glare and saw the red and blue flashing lights of a police cruiser.

"I called 911," Jack said. "Of course, you were doing pretty well on your own, baby doll."

Holly let out a shuddering sigh. "Good—they can take this creep off our hands."

And she hoped they locked him up and threw away the key. She also hoped Adam got everything he had coming to him, as well.

"What's going on here?" one officer called out.

"We caught our vandal," Jack told the cop.

The officer flashed his beam of light over the guy, then Jack and the lime green paint covering him from head to toe

208

and still dripping onto the pavement. "Hey, man, you're a little early for Halloween, aren't you?" He turned to his partner. "Get a load of this, Phillips."

The two cops were having a field day at Jack's expense—but Jack didn't care. They finally had the lowlife who'd been making Holly's life hell. He wanted to go to her and comfort her, but he couldn't even touch her without getting paint all over her.

"You okay?" he asked instead. "You look a little . . . green around the gills."

"So do you, Jack."

Jack looked down at the paint covering nearly every inch of him. He'd never wear green again—not any shade of it.

Ever.

The rest of the time was spent talking with the police, answering their questions, and swearing out a formal complaint. They both had the pleasure of seeing the creep handcuffed and placed in the backseat of the police cruiser.

While Holly finished up with the police, Jack headed across the street to his office and cleaned as much of the paint off as he could, found a set of clothes he kept there and quickly changed, then returned to Holly's lot. The police were just driving away with the vandal when he got back.

Holly had slumped against the door of one of her autos.

"Come on, I'll drive you home," he said.

"No, Jack. I'm fine. I'll drive myself."

Her voice was cool—and Jack caught the change in her mood. What the hell was wrong? She knew now, without a shadow of a doubt, that he hadn't been involved.

The police had the perpetrator and he'd given up the name of the man who'd given the order to cause Holly trouble. Adam, he was sure, would soon be in custody.

"Holly, what's wrong?" Maybe she was still in shock. He

couldn't blame her if she was.

He tried to go to her, put his arms around her, tell her everything was all right now, that it was over—but she pushed him away.

"I—I need some time to myself," she said and walked over to her Thunderbird and got in, leaving him standing there, wondering what the hell had happened.

Holly hadn't taken any calls for the past three days—except for the one from the police. They'd picked up Adam. He'd been living in Fort Worth, and after questioning, had finally admitted he'd hired the guy to do his dirty work.

Holly had had the misfortune of running into him at the police station. She'd been there for some questioning, Adam for detention, handcuffed and bitter, if the fiery glance he'd shot her in the back hallway of the station was any indication. She'd asked to use the restroom and had taken a wrong turn in finding it. Or maybe the wrong turn had been allowing her feelings for him to exist two years ago.

She tore her gaze away from his, feeling sullied, and escaped without a word spoken by either of them. But it would stay with her for far too long, she knew.

He'd been evening an old score with her, she supposed. But then she didn't really know how his mind worked, what he had been thinking. Only that he'd been set on revenge.

He'd made her life a living hell for months and nearly sent her company into bankruptcy. But the worst damage he'd done had been to her judgment. It was badly shaken, her already low trust quotient lower than ever.

She'd loved the man once, or thought she had. She'd trusted him, and he'd betrayed her, not just after her father's death, but now this second time.

She was certain he'd been the one behind the call from

the attorney, trying to buy her out. Probably with ill-gotten money. He'd stolen from her father—and once a thief, always a thief. When she hadn't tumbled to his price, he'd begun the whisper campaign against her and Hanford Motors.

It was why no one could find out who was spreading the rumors. They hadn't come from anyone local—but from someone in her past. At least someone she'd *thought* was in her past.

She'd underestimated Adam and the lengths he'd go to.

And it had been a big mistake.

One she'd never make again—with anyone.

This one had nearly cost her Hanford's.

She couldn't even allow Jack into her heart, despite the fact that he'd helped her. She'd seen the stunned look in his eyes when she'd pushed him away, but she couldn't explain, didn't know how to tell him what this had done to her.

Like a wounded animal all she could do was curl into herself, hold in her pain, her insecurity—and she didn't know if she'd ever be whole again.

Her judgment had been shot to pieces. She no longer trusted herself to make right choices about anything. Or anyone. She needed time. She needed to think.

And she needed to do that alone.

Life didn't allow a person many mistakes—and Holly was sure she'd already used up her share.

She placed T.R. in charge at Hanford's—while she nursed her faulty judgment, her injured pride.

She'd promised herself after Adam that she'd be cautious letting another man get close to her—but Jack had charmed his way into her life.

And then into her bed.

She had to hold onto her heart—or maybe she'd lost it to

him already. She didn't know. All she knew was that she was frightened of the future, of taking a wrong step.

Of taking *any* step.

Jack had spent the past week trying to see Holly. She hadn't come into the dealership, wouldn't answer her phone or her front door.

What the hell was wrong?

He'd spent a few nights on a barstool in a neighborhood bar, downing more beers than he should, trying to figure it all out. But all he knew was that he missed her like hell—and that he loved her.

The last realization had nearly knocked him to the floor. He'd been attracted to her from the first moment he saw her; he'd been infatuated; he'd been in lust.

Then love had stepped in and knocked him six ways from Sunday.

He wasn't sure when it had happened. The night he'd made love to her? Or before that? All he knew was it was ingrained deeply in him now—and there'd never be another woman for him but Holly.

He closed up Mad Jack's, gave a hopeful glance across the street, but Holly's car wasn't there. T.R. had been in charge of the day-to-day operations lately.

For a moment fury laced his insides.

She trusted T.R.—but not him.

Damn! He should just forget her, thank his lucky stars that he'd averted marriage and commitment, babies and the proverbial picket fence. He was free to fix up the ranch, or sell out and move on, build up Mad Jack's or leave the whole street to Holly.

He couldn't drive the MG anymore. Whenever he even glanced at it, it reminded him of her. Maybe if he decided to move on he'd tie a giant ribbon around it and leave it on her doorstep.

He opened the door to the big Dually he'd tried to sell to the guy he'd sent over to Holly's place. Good enough, he thought. It would work great on the ranch—much better than the little MG, anyway. He crawled up into the cab and slammed the door hard enough to shake the windows.

Women were a confusing breed.

Maybe he'd go to the bar, drown his pride and his sorrows. Though that sure hadn't worked for him yet. Maybe he'd go to the ranch, sit on the porch and look at the stars. Maybe he'd just drive, not caring where he ended up, and never come back.

He chose the bar, swung himself up onto a stool at the end of the counter and ordered his usual. There was a crowd tonight. A band played the usual country songs and he watched as couples danced. It was Saturday—date night in Texas.

He recalled dancing with Holly, holding her close, breathing in the heady scent of her. He wished she were here—he'd lead her onto the floor, drape her hands around his neck, hold her at the waist and never let her go. They'd close the place, then he'd take her home to his bed and make love to her.

They seemed good together; they fit like two parts of a whole. If he conjured up his idea of a dream woman, that woman would be Holly. She filled his dreams at night and his thoughts during the day.

He downed the rest of his beer and ordered another. But no amount of drinking could dissipate his pain. He killed some time at the bar, knowing it was too early to go home. At home he'd be alone with his thoughts.

Here at least there was activity—something, no matter

how inane, to focus his mind on. But soon even that failed to occupy his attention.

He tossed a few bills on the bar and left.

Holly's friend Leah called her Monday and insisted on dragging her out of her house for lunch and an afternoon of shopping. Holly begged off from the shopping trip. It held no appeal to her. Besides, there wasn't anything she needed.

But she did have to eat, so she took Leah up on her invitation.

They chose a chick restaurant, as Leah liked to call it. A tearoom, filled with antiques, starched white tablecloths and fragrant-smelling flowers on each table. It was always one of Holly's favorites.

And she knew she wouldn't run into any males from her life, past or present.

Leah leaned forward after they'd ordered. "Tell me what happened with the vandal. Did you and Jack really catch the guy red-handed?"

Holly didn't want to talk about Jack, but she knew word of the takedown and the arrest had rippled through the small town faster than the bad rumor that had very nearly destroyed her.

"It was something I don't ever want to go through again," she said. "And I was glad to have Jack there. I couldn't have handled the creep myself."

"Oh, Holly." Leah's frown showed her worry. "And Adam was behind it?"

That bit of information wasn't as well known as the arrest, but many who had known Holly and Adam were aware of the circumstances. "Yes—I'm afraid so. Adam's a malicious man. How could I ever have fallen for him?"

214

"Don't blame yourself, Holly. Adam fooled a lot of people. He was a charmer."

Like Jack Murdock, Holly thought.

But Jack was a mistake she wouldn't compound by seeing him again. She hadn't gone back to work yet, where she'd see him and Mad Jack's across the street—but she was getting stronger. Just being here with Leah showed she was ready to take a few baby steps.

"I told the police I suspected Adam had been skimming money from Hanford's when he worked for my father. They suggested I go over the books and they'd be happy to slap a few extra charges on him. I've gone over the old accounting records and could tell my father moved a lot of cars, but the cash end just didn't add up. I talked to Brewer Phillips about it and he offered to loan me the accountant he used to have. He said if there'd been any cooking of the books the guy could find it."

"Are you going to do it?"

"Yes. I'm not sure what the statute of limitations is on the crime—if there is a crime—but I have to know the extent of Adam's treachery. And prosecute, if possible."

"Good. I see some of the old fight in you again," Leah said.

Their croissant sandwiches arrived then and both were quiet for a while as they sampled the food. Leah took a sip of her iced tea, then set the glass down and looked over at Holly. "So, tell me about Jack Murdock," she said.

Holly glanced up at her friend and wondered how she could steer her away from *that* topic. "What about him?"

"You spent hours with him on the lot. I want details."

Details. When it came to Jack she didn't know what to list as details. "Well, the poor guy did end up with a bucket of lime green paint hefted at him."

"And he probably still looked gorgeous." Her friend gave a long breathy sigh.

Holly rolled her eyes. "I was too upset to notice."

"I can't imagine what circumstances it would take to make me blind to that guy's looks."

"Leah, you're a married woman."

"I may be married, but marriage didn't blur my eyesight. You, Holly, are single—and could use a man in your life. Why not the gorgeous Jack Murdock?"

Holly was quiet for a moment. "What if I make the same mistake?" Her question was low as if voicing it to herself—and she probably was.

But Leah heard her anyway. "Give yourself some time and space—and then put Adam where he belongs—in your past, with lesson learned."

She had learned her lesson all right. And now caution guided her every step.

And mistrust.

Just when she thought she was finally becoming secure in her emotions, when she thought she could be tumbling head over heels in love with Jack, Adam came back to remind her of her mistake—and make her doubt her judgment all over again.

"No woman likes to be played for a fool," she said quietly.

Why hadn't she seen through Adam? And what might she be missing with Jack? She'd always considered herself savvy—but now she wasn't so sure.

Now she just felt . . . foolish.

"Of course not, but don't tar every man you meet with the same brush, Holly. You'll only end up alone and bitter."

Bitter? She'd carried her bitterness over Adam around with her for a long time—until Jack made her forget just a little. She'd been on her way to putting it aside for good when all this had happened.

How could she trust Jack? How could she trust any man after this? She knew Leah was right, she needed to put aside her fear—but how did she get there from here?

Just then the waitress came by with the dessert cart and Holly smiled as Leah drooled at the sight of the selections.

"I'll take the one with no calories. How about you, Holly?"

Holly grinned. From what she could see of the rich desserts there wasn't a single item with fewer than a thousand calories each. "None for me," she said. "But go ahead. I'll have a mocha latte, while you satisfy your sweet tooth."

Leah chose a big slice of lemon meringue pie and sampled a bite, nearly purring in contentment. The waitress returned with a refill on Leah's iced tea and brought Holly's mocha latte.

Holly warmed her hands through the cup, barely noticing the rich smell that normally tempted her taste buds. The little tearoom had good food, but her croissant sandwich may as well have been cardboard with mayo for all her awareness of what she'd eaten.

Still, she'd finished off half the sandwich, which was more than she'd gotten down in a week. She hadn't had an appetite or the desire to see anyone.

That night on her lot, believing that Adam was in her past and couldn't harm her, had changed everything for her.

"You're brooding, Holly."

She glanced up. Leah had polished off her dessert and was studying her intently. Was she brooding? She'd been doing a lot of that lately.

"I—I'm sorry. I guess I'm not very good company. Not that I haven't enjoyed today. Thank you for dragging me out."

"So when are you going to rejoin the human race?" Her friend's look nailed her to the fancy chair she was sitting on.

Holly sighed. She couldn't hide forever—she knew that. "This week—though it will be gender-specific. I'm not ready to trust with my heart just yet."

Maybe she never would be.

Hot damn!

Jack saw the Thunderbird across the street at Hanford Motors. That meant only one thing—Holly was there. And he was sure as hell going to see her.

She'd ignored him for the past week and a half, hiding out at home—and out of his reach. But this afternoon, for whatever reason, she'd put in an appearance at her lot. He hadn't forgotten the way she felt in his arms, how perfectly their bodies fit together. She was his.

Whether she knew it or not.

He'd never had to woo a woman this long or this hard. Forget that. He'd never *cared* to woo a woman this long or this hard.

Until Holly.

He ducked into the small bathroom in his trailer office and checked out his looks in the mirror. A half-moment later he had his hair slicked back and his tie straightened in a business-like knot. He scurried back to his office chair and snatched up his sports jacket from the back of his desk chair.

But with an arm halfway into his sleeve he ripped off the garment. The jacket wouldn't do. It was a colorful watermelon red. And Jack wanted to look good.

He tossed it aside, sleeve turned inside out.

Okay—he wouldn't wear a jacket. He'd go for the casual look, he thought, and loosened his tie.

Forget the tie, too.

It was canary gold with little racecars dotting it. Also poor taste. He stripped it off and loosened the top button of his denim shirt.

One more trip to the bathroom mirror told him this was better.

She might even be swept off her feet by his handsome good looks.

A man could hope.

He locked up his office and skirted through the traffic racing along Woodland Avenue and over to Holly's place. His pulse was rearing like a wild horse. He had to calm down. When he reached the front door he took three deep breaths, pulled open the showroom door, and bolted inside.

"Your Boss Lady in her office?" he asked T.R. who presided over the place with wary quietude.

"She doesn't want to be disturbed, Murdock—and you're the most disturbed man I know."

Jack gave a low chuckle. T.R. didn't like him one bit. Some things never changed.

Her office door was closed. Jack rapped his knuckles on the wood and heard nothing from inside. He rapped again, harder this time. When Holly was knee-deep in work she wouldn't hear a volcano if it erupted beside her.

"Come in—and this better be important," came her determined voice.

She was in fighting mode—just the way he liked her.

He opened the door and swung it inward. She gave a soft sigh when she saw him and picked up an inventory printout. "I'm very busy, Jack. Come back next year."

Yep—she was in fighting form all right.

He noticed the blue smudges beneath her eyes. She probably hadn't been sleeping well—and neither had he. Still she looked beautiful to him. In fact, he couldn't imagine any way she could look that she wouldn't seem beautiful to him.

He perched on the edge of her desk. "You've been dodging me, Countess, and I want to know why."

She glanced down at the paperwork in front of her. "I've just been busy."

"Busy?" That was a load of crock—and he knew it. She'd been holed up in that house of hers as if she were fearful of something.

"I'm sorry I forgot to thank you for all you did that night," she said softly. "Catching the vandal, finding out who was behind everything that had been happening at Hanford's."

He frowned. "I didn't come here for a damned thank you, Holly." She'd plain been avoiding him. Of course, in all honesty, she'd been avoiding everybody.

And he wanted to know why.

"Look, Jack, I just needed some space after all that's happened."

Maybe Jack did deserve an explanation of why she was running, Holly thought, but she didn't know how to make him understand how unsure she was of herself. How Adam had knocked her legs out from under her with what he'd done. That she no longer dared rely on her instincts, wasn't even sure she could make it through this afternoon, much less the rest of her life.

She couldn't trust herself not to fall into Jack's arms—which, she realized, was where she wanted to be.

The expression on his face told her he wasn't about to let her go until she'd explained why she'd been dodging him. He was waiting, his blue eyes dark with hurt.

She didn't want to hurt him—but she didn't want to be hurt either.

And she had the feeling that if she didn't find some way to resist his infectious charm, she'd be making a dicey mistake.

Adam had left her life rocky, her self-confidence shredded and her trust level non-existent.

But maybe she did owe Jack an answer.

She'd been grateful for his help on her lot. And she knew she had hurt him. She'd seen the haunted look in his eyes.

Holly glanced at her watch. It was nearly four o'clock and she'd promised T.R. she'd finish up some work. "Give me an hour to finish up this stack of invoices and then we'll go somewhere and talk," she said.

Chapter Fifteen

Jack closed up and drove over to Hanford's. He wasn't giving Holly a chance to sneak out on him.

"Ready?" he asked, sticking his head in her office doorway.

She looked tired and he longed to go to her, drag her into his arms and kiss away every sign of fatigue. She tossed the last of her work into her Out Basket with a sigh, and gathered up her purse. "Yes," she said, "I'm ready."

He had Kim Loo's in mind for dinner. It was her favorite Chinese restaurant in town. He helped her into the red MG and shut the door, then scrambled around to his side and crawled in behind the wheel.

"I thought someone would have bought the MG by now," she said.

Jack's reply was terse. "It's not for sale."

"Why not? It's the best car on your lot."

He frowned. "I don't care if it's the *only* car on my lot. It won't have a price tag on it."

The car belonged to Holly. He thought of her every time he looked at it, imagined her sweet scent clinging to every corner and fiber of it. He saw her rich brown hair blowing in the created breeze, remembered every time she sat in that little bucket seat or behind the wheel, putting the little car through its paces, her green eyes lit with excitement.

And she'd have talked him into a hot, bargain price for it by now if all this skullduggery hadn't happened to her and Hanford's, he knew.

"You look tired," he said. "What about just getting Kim Loo's to go and taking it to the ranch?" he asked.

"My place is closer," she said.

Anywhere was fine with Jack. He got on his cell phone, punched in his speed dial number for the Chinese restaurant and ordered everything he knew Holly liked. By the time he reached the take-out window the food was ready to go. "Mmmm, this smells good," she said, grabbing the multitude of bags so Jack could drive. "I didn't realize I was so hungry."

"Think you can hold out until we get to your place?"

She dug through the bags, looking for something to sample, but at his question, she pinched the top of them together and smiled over at him. "Afraid I'll eat all your favorites before we get there?"

Damn! He was crazy in love with this woman. One soft smile from her was easily his undoing. "Not hardly. With your puny appetite you couldn't eat half my favorites."

One dark eyebrow rose. "I'll show you who has a puny appetite, Jack Murdock. You may just have to drive back to Kim Loo's for *your* order—this one's all mine."

He laughed easily with her. Some of her old fight was still there. Or maybe he just brought it out in her. He liked her going for his jugular.

She was a worthy opponent—and he'd never had so much fun tangling with an adversary before. She was easily his equal when it came to a good fight.

Jack pulled into her driveway and killed the engine. He reached for the carryout bags as Holly dug in her purse for her house key.

He ran around the car to open the door for her but she was already out and heading for the front door. He couldn't help noticing that trim little backside of hers as she made it up the porch steps. He'd like to slip that skinny little dress off her and kiss her all over. He wanted to make love to her and never stop.

Holly set everything out on the coffee table and took a seat on the floor.

The skinny little dress would have to wait.

He'd ordered a bottle of white wine from Kim Loo's and Holly sent him into the kitchen for a corkscrew and two wine glasses. He rummaged around in her cabinets and found them, and also two plates, then returned to the living room and took a seat beside her on the floor. She looked beat—but it failed to mar her sweet beauty. Nothing could mar that.

Jack popped the cork on the wine and poured some into the goblets, then set one in front of Holly.

"Thanks," she said, picking up the glass and taking a dainty sip.

Jack wanted to down his in a single gulp, but he needed a clear head so after one swallow he set the goblet down and tried some of the food. It was delicious as only Kim Loo could make it. Holly was eating hers, though slowly. But at least she was eating.

Her living room was softly lit by one low lamp. The light cast creamy shadows over her face and he noted the blue shadows beneath her eyes. He wanted to kiss them away. But Holly wouldn't go for that, he was sure.

She finally shoved her plate away and Jack did the same with his.

"Okay, talk," he said. "What's going on, Holly? We catch the guy behind your trouble and then you do a vanishing act."

"I know and I'm sorry."

"C'mon, Holly. Sorry doesn't cut it. I want answers."

"Don't order me around, Jack." She leaned back against the base of the sofa; her legs curled under her and her eyes were lit with green fire.

"I wasn't ordering, I just need to know what's going on in that head of yours," he said. He'd been worried as hell about her. Something was wrong—and he didn't want it to be.

Holly saw the pain her sharp words had caused and she hated herself for hurting Jack. But it had been a knee-jerk reaction. A bad memory planted in her brain of Adam's threats and bullying. He had affected her more than she realized. And seeing him at the police station, his eyes dark and treacherous as their glances met, hadn't helped.

She'd been hiding out, licking her emotional wounds while her friends—and one adversary—had been worried about her. She remembered she'd promised Jack an explanation—and she knew she owed him one.

She took a slow sip of her wine for courage and met the soft gaze in his eyes. The warmth in his eyes, more than the wine, gave her the strength she needed.

"I made a bad mistake with Adam," she began. "I thought he was out of my life, but he wasn't." And now she knew he wouldn't be for a long time. The sight of him had brought everything back to her in startling reality.

She took another sip of her wine and went on. "I thought I loved him once, thought he loved me. But as it turned out he only wanted one thing. And that was Hanford's. I just came as part of the deal."

"Then the man was a fool as well as a louse. But we got him now, sweetheart—he can't hurt you again."

The softness of Jack's words made her want to believe him, but Adam's specter still lingered, doing its damage, damage to

225

her and to any future she might have or want to have.

With Jack.

"No, Jack—you don't understand. I believed he was gone from my life, that he was part of my past. I trusted that all this was behind me—but it never was. He came back once more—for revenge. And I didn't see it either time. He took something from me, and that something is trust in my own judgment. I can no longer rely on it when it comes to making decisions, making a deal at Hanford's or trusting any man I meet and think I care about—like you. I can't trust in a future for myself."

"I won't hurt you, Holly. I could never do that."

Her voice quivered. "Adam said that to me too—but he did hurt me, is still hurting me."

He'd tried to crush her spirit, steal her company—and she was sure he'd taken from her father as well. But from her father, he'd only stolen money. From her he'd stolen more, he'd stolen her trust and her belief in herself. She couldn't risk going through something like that again. Not ever.

Jack bristled. He was angry, she could tell. "Damn it, Holly—I'm not Adam Stone."

Her gaze raked over him, taking in his broad shoulders squared to do battle if that's what it took to win her over, the scorn in his voice, the determination in his eyes. No—he wasn't Adam Stone.

But who was he?

Someone she loved—but was afraid to admit it.

If she did he might turn into someone else, someone like Adam.

Or worse.

"Jack, I'm sorry—but I need time and I need space right now. This . . . well, a lot has happened to me and I'm not sure of who I am or what I want."

226

"So you intend to hide away from me, from everyone who loves you. Why, Holly? So no one hurts you again. Well, babe, life is a series of hurts."

"Jack, please understand—"

Jack understood one thing. Holly didn't trust him enough to let herself love him. Maybe she never would. His heart ached like he carried the weight of the world around in it.

He didn't think he'd ever fall in love, and now that he had, the object of his love didn't want him.

Life was a bitch. He might as well be back in New York, playing with money on Wall Street. It was a cold job. Money couldn't warm a man's bed at night—and he realized now that that's why he'd come here to Texas.

He'd wanted something meaningful in his life.

He'd wanted a woman he loved and who loved him enough to snuggle beside him, to wake up with him in the morning, wake up with a beautiful day ahead of them, wake up with hopes and dreams, a future to share.

As much as he wanted Holly to be that woman, she wasn't.

Maybe she never could be.

"Space—well if that's the way you want it, you've got it, babe." Space was another word for *shove off, buster.*

And that's what Jack intended to do.

"Please, Jack, try to understand."

He got up from the floor and their dinner. Understand? He understood all right. Holly wasn't the only one who could make mistakes.

He'd made a beaut of one—falling in love with a woman he couldn't have. But wanted so damned bad, he ached for just the touch of her body. His heart crushed, his future, *their* future, nonexistent, Jack strode to the front door. He gave no backward glance as he opened it, he couldn't, wouldn't, or he'd shatter into a million broken pieces.

Maybe he already had.

Holly cleaned up the remainder of their dinner, rinsed out the wine glasses and climbed the stairs to her bedroom. The room had never felt as empty as it did tonight.

The moment Jack had left she'd wanted to go to him, call him back, tell him she was sorry she'd sent him away. But she couldn't do that. Whenever she'd led with her heart, her heart came away bruised and battered.

She wasn't strong enough to risk that.

Not yet.

Maybe not ever.

Jack wasn't Adam—Jack had told her that, and she knew it. But Jack could hurt her if she let herself love him, if she didn't keep her defenses tightly in place, her emotions in check.

But she knew she did love Jack. She wanted to deny it— but she couldn't. She wanted him in her life, but her heart wasn't ready. She wasn't strong enough to risk her feelings. Adam had hurt her, but Jack had the power to devastate her if he chose to.

Maybe things were better this way, her little company on one side of the street and Jack and his place on the other.

He was angry with her. But Holly knew only one thing, self-protection. That was her ally, along with mistrust, suspicion and caution.

But they made lonely bedfellows.

Jack carried a beer out to the porch and proceeded to nurse his wounds. The night and the ranch seemed to mock him. He was here alone under the night's brilliant moon.

He'd loved this place once. It had beckoned him to buy it

and make it his. Something tangible, something that would last, something he could build a future on. But there was no future for him without Holly in it.

Not here.

Maybe not anywhere.

Damn, but he loved her, had imagined her here with him at the ranch, in his bed, her scent and her touch making this a home, not just a lonely ranch house.

He took a long swallow of his beer, propped his booted feet on the porch railing and wanted to bay at the moon like a wounded animal. He hadn't even gotten the chance to tell her he loved her. But then she wouldn't have believed he meant it.

Damn, but he wanted to take Adam Stone and wring the life out of him for what he had done to Holly, was still doing as insidiously as if he were somewhere besides the county jail.

The man would get a stiff fine and a slap on the wrist for what he'd done to Hanford's, but it would be Holly and Jack who'd live with the consequences forever.

She didn't trust Jack not to hurt her, to love her the way she should be loved, wholly and completely.

And he couldn't convince her.

She didn't think he understood what this treachery had done to her, how it shook her faith once again—but Jack understood only too well. She wasn't going to give Jack a chance.

She couldn't trust him.

And that's what hurt him the most.

When morning came Jack awoke with half a dozen empty beer bottles lined up like crows on the porch railing, one whopper of a headache and a crick in his neck that promised to become permanent.

Other than that nothing had changed.

He didn't even want to go into Mad Jack's. He'd see Holly across the street and his heart would split in two. Would she hurt just a little for him, for what would never be?

She'd manage, he knew. Holly was a survivor. Jack had always thought he was a survivor too—but now he had his doubts. It would be hell trying to get over this woman, if he ever could.

He heard a whinny from the stables and knew he had to feed and water the horses. He dragged his stiff and battered body out of the porch swing and stumbled in that direction.

"What's wrong, old girl?" he said to Daisy. "You get up on the wrong side of the stall this morning? Well, you aren't the only one." He gave her a pat on her nose and put out feed for her, Geronimo and Brownie, the other horse he'd bought.

His mind began calculating how much this place would bring him, the house, the livestock. And then there was Mad Jack's, his meager inventory.

Enough.

It would bring enough for him to get the hell out of Dodge.

He didn't know where he'd go. He only knew he had to get away to somewhere—somewhere that wouldn't remind him constantly of Holly. Maybe he'd go back to Wall Street.

The action and the stress of the place left little time to think.

He'd wanted more from life, but without Holly in that life, it wouldn't be worth living. Maybe he'd go home and see his mother—and visit his sisters and the little rug rat nieces and nephews he'd accrued over the past few years.

No, he thought, not his sisters. Their happiness would only mock him. But his mother. Maybe he'd even tell her about the woman he'd fallen in love with, the woman he couldn't have, but would love forever. She'd understand.

His mother always did.

Beyond that he'd go where the wind blew him.

Holly hadn't seen Jack for a week and a half. He'd come in to Mad Jack's but she'd noticed he'd spent only part of his day there selling cars. Maybe the ranch was keeping him extra busy.

He hadn't dropped in to see her the way he often did; he hadn't called or tried to see her in any way.

She missed seeing him, missed their sparring matches, missed his kisses—missed everything about him. He'd bowed out of her life—but that, she knew, was her own fault. She'd sent him away. And now she wondered if that had been the wrong thing to do.

Jack had never hurt her. He'd been stiff competition for her, yes, but Hanford's was once again holding its own. And Holly was relieved.

Still she missed Jack wrangling with her, keeping her on her toes with his television commercials and the drag-in-the-customer sales he put on. She didn't even mind his gargantuan sign anymore. Just his ugly jackets—though, she had to admit, she hadn't seen him wear any wild ones lately.

Not that she'd been looking, of course.

She drew into her lot and parked her Thunderbird in her parking space, gathered up her purse and her briefcase and came around to the front of the building. T.R. was staring across the street at Mad Jack's. *Oh, no!* she thought. Had Jack done something outrageous again?

Something that would spell trouble for her?

"Thought you'd want to see this, Holly," T.R. said and pointed across the street.

Holly was afraid to look.

"What's he done now?" she asked.

"Take a look. I think you'll be happy about this one," T.R. returned.

She drew a deep breath and slowly glanced over at Mad Jack's. But Holly wasn't happy about what she saw. Her heart plunged to her toes. Jack had a large sign strung up across his lot.

Going Out Of Business!!

"We won't have to worry about him stealing our business any more," T.R. said.

Holly couldn't breathe. She could only stand there speechless and stare.

"Ain't that a pretty sight," T.R. went on, totally unaware of her shock, her pain.

"Excuse me," she managed to get out coherently. "I—I have work to do."

It was a lame pretext, but she had to get away before she fell apart, before she collapsed in front of him, before he saw the tears gather in her eyes.

Her legs were shaky as she made her way inside and into her office. She slammed the door, then stepped to the front window and parted the blinds that she'd kept solemnly closed for the past week and a half so she wouldn't see Jack, wouldn't be tempted to ask him to come back, to make love to her the way her body wanted.

Yes, the sign was there, swaying in the soft summer breeze. She blinked back tears and looked again, hoping it was a mirage, a trick of the eye—but of course it was still there.

Maybe Jack didn't want her after all. Maybe he'd just been toying with her affections, making her love him—when all the time he hadn't intended to stay around.

As the morning wore on, a thousand questions came to

mind, questions she had no answers to. Her heart felt like it was breaking in two. She longed to pick up the phone and call him, ask him what was going on. She wanted to run across the street to his lot and read the answers in his eyes.

In the end she did none of those things.

She spent the day trying to work—but couldn't find the will or the strength. She ate her lunch from the vending machine, though most of that she tossed in the waste receptacle because she had no appetite. She avoided T.R. because she didn't want him to see how affected she was that Jack was pulling up stakes.

T.R. didn't like Jack, she knew, and had no idea that Holly had fallen, and fallen hard for the man.

By closing time Holly had a major headache. She'd gone into the small bathroom off her office, and with the door locked, had cried her eyes out more than a dozen times.

Jack didn't love her. Not enough to fight for her. Not enough to stick around. Not enough to wait until she was steady again and could trust her own heart.

At six o'clock she noticed it was quiet on her lot. Everyone had gone home. And Holly was alone. Maybe she'd go across the street and confront Jack, find out why he was folding.

Maybe he was giving up his lot to spend more time on the ranch.

She clung to this last shred of hope—though she didn't really believe that was the case. Jack would have told her.

Or would he have?

He'd made no effort to see her, she remembered.

She cracked the blinds at the window and peered across the street. The lot was closed up tight. Holly let the blinds snap back into place, gathered up her purse, locked her desk drawer and headed out into the evening. Her heart was aching. She didn't want Jack to leave. She couldn't bear it if he did.

She nearly tripped over it.

The red MG.

It was parked outside her showroom door, keys on the driver's seat and a note on the windshield. Her hand shook as she reached for the note tucked securely beneath the wiper blade.

She swallowed hard, and with fingers trembling, she opened the folded sheet of paper.

"The car's for you," it read. *"I couldn't bring myself to sell it."*

Tears welled up in her eyes. Her heart hammered like a jackhammer that had gone berserk.

Why had Jack given her the little car?

A thousand thoughts raced through her mind, making her brain hurt and her headache throb worse than ever. She needed answers—and there was only one man who could give them to her.

Jack.

She opened the door to the MG, tossed in her purse, then climbed in behind the wheel. The interior glowed, the dash polished, the seats gleaming and looking like new. She'd wanted the car—and Jack knew it. But she didn't want it like this.

Without Jack.

How dare he do this to her? Give her the car, then walk away. She wanted Jack, wanted him more than she'd ever wanted any man before.

And now she was losing him.

He was leaving her the MG—and a bundle of heartache to endure.

The ride to the ranch seemed long and endless, when in fact, Jack's place was only a few miles out of town. Thoughts tumbled over themselves in her head. Every sweet thing Jack had ever done played through Holly's mind.

And what had she done?

She'd accused him of being behind her every problem.

He'd tried to help—but she'd been too stubborn and too frightened to let her heart trust in his goodness.

He'd irritated her beyond belief in the beginning, but even then he'd captivated her soul with his charm. She hadn't trusted her feelings, hadn't trusted him, letting the past frighten her, her past with Adam color the present.

And destroy her future.

She saw Jack through a skewered prism of suspicion and doubt. But her heart and her hormones betrayed her over and over again. Until she'd fallen in love with him.

She turned onto the road to the ranch and saw the sign before she even reached the drive.

For Sale.

Her heart, the last tiny shred of hope that Jack wasn't truly leaving, sank like a stone.

She'd lost him, lost the best thing that had ever happened to her, and all because of her foolish fears. She stopped the car in the drive's entrance, her hands shaking on the wheel, her legs trembling, her heart sick and heavy. Tears stung her eyes and trickled down her cheeks. She had only herself to blame.

With her heart heavy, she drove the final distance up the drive.

She'd return the car—she couldn't keep it.

Jack came out from the stables. Her heart turned over and her pulses throbbed painfully. He looked gorgeous; backlit by the setting sun and tears fell afresh down her cheeks. For what seemed like forever he stood there and stared, as if she were an apparition, as if she was the last person in the world he expected to see.

Finally he moved toward the car, his gait that easy lope she remembered.

Her throat clotted with pain.

He opened her car door and she tried to step out, hoping her shaky legs would support her. "It's true then—you're leaving?"

Holly knew the answer—and wished she'd never asked it.

He gave a shrug of his wide shoulders. "I thought it best—under the circumstances."

Holly crumpled against the car door. How could she tell him now that she loved him? That she'd made the biggest mistake of her life in not trusting him?

"I have to return the car," she said hollowly, "I can't keep it."

"Of course you can. It's yours, it's always been yours—from the first moment I saw you in it."

His eyes held a bittersweet smile, though none showed on his lips. What had she done to him, to a love that could have been—except for her stubbornness?

She couldn't keep the car. "No, Jack." She handed him the keys. "If you'll just drive me home . . ."

Jack wanted to drag her into the house and make love to her in that old four-poster bed. Did she really want him to drive her home and forget he loved her?

He couldn't do that.

"I love you, Holly—that's why I'm leaving. I can't stay here and see you every day and know that you don't love me."

She turned her face to his. The setting sun glistened on the tears shining in her eyes. It gave him a moment of hope—but he'd moved past hope last week.

He'd made his decision to sell out and to leave then. His heart could take no more longing or wishing. He had to be practical.

"What did you say?" she asked.

He sighed. "I said that I'm leaving."

"No—before that."

He paused and looked into her open face. Nothing was hidden there now—as it so often was before. Her feelings were exposed for him to see—and damn it all, if that ridiculous hope didn't spring up to choke him once again.

His words were strangled. "I said, I love you."

"I love you, too."

Jack had to listen hard to be sure what she'd said. Her voice was a whisper and he thought for a moment that he'd heard only what he'd *wanted* to hear.

"Don't leave. I hurt you, Jack. I hurt both of us—but I don't want you to go. I love you."

The second 'I love you' sounded like a shout. He'd heard it loud and clear—and he'd never let her take it back.

Jack wanted to roar with happiness, but before he could, Holly was in his arms. Her body felt wonderful and oh-so-right up against his.

"I want you to stay," her voice trembled. "I was so miserable when I saw your sign over Mad Jack's and the For Sale sign on the ranch."

He soothed her with kisses. "If you want me, Holly, you couldn't get rid of me with a shotgun."

"I want you, Jack. I think I always have."

He picked her up and carried her up to the front door of the ranch, then inside and up the stairs to the bedroom. He had plans for her in that big four-poster bed of his.

He stood her on her feet beside it.

"Marry me, Holly. Be my wife, my lover, my life."

His breath caught and held until he heard her answer, terrified that there was a hitch, that she wouldn't be his after all.

"Yes, Jack, I'll marry you."

Jack gave her his best charming smile. He loved this woman. And she loved him. Nothing could be better than that.

Nothing at all.

Epilogue

Jack grabbed Holly's hand as they ran toward the red MG in a hail of bridal rice.

With the gaiety and well wishes of the wedding crowd at the reception ringing in their ears, he crammed the little car into gear and they raced off. Finally he'd have his new bride all to himself.

Laughing, Holly brushed rice from the shoulders of his black tux, then shook the stuff from the voluminous yards of white satin in her skirt.

"I can't wait to get you out of that dress, Holly Hanford Murdock," he said, offering her his most charming grin. He'd thought of little else since he watched her glide down the aisle on T.R.'s arm earlier. The man had given his blessing the day Jack closed his business and returned Luther to the fold of Hanford Motors.

"You'll have to exert a ton of patience, Jack. It took Leah twenty minutes just to hook the trail of tiny buttons down the back."

"That's because she was excited for you," he said.

Everyone was excited for them, wishing them many years of wedded bliss.

Jack intended to do his part about the wedded bliss just as soon as he got her to the ranch.

Holly was his—and he was the happiest man on the face of the earth.

He couldn't wait to get her naked and into his big four-poster bed. *Their* four-poster bed now. Holly fit at the ranch. He'd realized that from the first moment he saw her there. Not that she was giving up Hanford Motors. She wasn't. In fact, her business was better than ever.

She'd taken some of Jack's inventory of autos and Brewer the remainder. Brewer had decided his son needed a little on-the-job training in the art of salesmanship and good will—so he was back at the helm. At least temporarily.

After what seemed like forever they arrived at the ranch and Jack carried his bride over the threshold. Her arms were wound around his neck, soft and sweet. He kissed her sultry mouth, then wished he hadn't—at least not until he'd gotten her out of that dress.

"You can put me down now," she said. "We're over the threshold."

"Oh, no—I have plans for you, sweetheart."

He carried her into the bedroom and laid her on the big four-poster bed. Holly giggled. He'd never have believed this woman could giggle, but it was definitely a giggle. And Jack loved the sound. He loved everything about her.

Except maybe for those buttons.

He held her to him and tried to undo them with his big clumsy fingers.

"Don't say I didn't warn you," she said.

"Quit nuzzling my neck, woman, or I'll never get this done."

Cursing the sadistic designer who'd come up with this idea for a wedding gown he undid the last troublesome button and slipped his bride out of it. Holly was worth the wait, the prize beneath the satin. And he intended to show her—now.

And every day for the rest of their lives.

About the Author

Gayle Kasper lives in Santa Fe, New Mexico with her husband and one very spoiled poodle. She's been writing romances for 15 years. Her first manuscript was a finalist in the Romance Writers of America's Golden Heart contest and went on to be published by Harlequin Temptation in 1990. Since then she's added ten more romances to her list of published works. She loves seeing her books in print and receiving foreign copies of them, which have been translated into German, French, Italian, Swedish, Dutch and Japanese. When she's not writing she loves reading, shopping and playing tourist in and around Santa Fe. Gayle loves hearing from her readers and you can e-mail her at readermail@juno.com.